# Shifting Passions

## Arian Mabe

This collection of erotic stories focuses on males and transformation.

The collection includes: male/solo scenes, gay sex, transformation, masturbation, arousal, anal, oral and public play.

# Table of Contents

# Feline
# Transformation

Rae bit his lip, sitting on his bed in nothing more than his boxer briefs, though the husky should not have concerned himself too much about his state of undress. Of course, the curtains were closed tightly against the outside world and a chilly winter night, the husky's black-furred tail tucked down, even with the natural curl trying to ping it back up again. It was not a natural position for Rae to hold his tail in, though the dog was more than a little anxious about what he was about to do.

"Really… I'm gonna…try?"

His lips quirked in a smile that disappeared as quickly as it appeared. Rae whined faintly, his tail trying to wag, though the dimness of his bedroom was not his focus as he took the small bottle in his paw. His white-furred fingers curled around it, claws rapping faintly on the glass, though he didn't need to be too careful with it. It was a single-use potion, after all, and he was going to take it all for twenty-four hours of change.

He wanted to say something funny like, "bottoms up," but he couldn't get it out and, in the end, just shrugged and tipped the potion down his throat, folding his black lips around the narrow neck of it. A drop of bubbling, clear potion fizzed on his lips as if it was trying to escape, but he swept his tongue quickly along his lower lip to make sure that every last drop was captured.

That was how it was supposed to be, after all, panting, whimpering, letting it all wash and roll through him, all so very deliciously. He grunted, something lurching in his stomach, though it was not that the potion wasn't sitting right in his stomach.

Rae groaned, the potion slipping from his fingers. He panted lightly, the husky's tail quivering, though he did not even dare wag it.

An escape…of a kind. It would ease through him, in time, allowing him to take on a new form and body, if only for a bit, but it was right, yes, it was chosen.

And that was just why he leaned back on the bed, his head tipped back, lips parted slightly. His tongue fluttered back and forth very faintly with every breath, though remained caged by his pearly white teeth, the sharper canines that would, soon, become a little lighter and a little finer.

They would all be such in time, yes, though his flesh bubbled and rippled, leaving a strange pushing and pulling sensation rising from within him. His stomach churned and Rae sucked in a breath the best that he could, though it was still not enough to satisfy the clamping tightness of his lungs.

Yet such a change was not meant to come slowly, no, not at all, not as it snarled and snapped within him, as if the transformation itself was far more feral and wilder than anything Rae had ever experienced. He didn't know what to think, what to feel, not as he grunted, the pressure increasing as if he was being squeezed all over by invisible paws clamping down on his arms, his legs, around his waist, his chest and more. His tail tried to lash but it was slimming down already, his black and white fur blending together into a light grey with darker stripes.

"Mmmmm…"

Although Rae really had no reason to blush, he was still hot around the face and down his neck. He was alone there and no one was going to come in and disturb him, allowing him to truly take in the peace of his transformation, licking his lips, even as his face crunched and crackled lightly across his jaw and cheekbones.

Apparently, he was not going to stay canine, he thought with a leap of his heart, letting his tongue flutter, becoming thinner, lighter, a little raspier. He ran it experimentally around the inside of his teeth, feeling it to be a little rougher than it had been before, though there were no anthros that stayed true to their earlier ancestry and heritage in its entirety.

So, a feline tongue would never be rough enough on an anthro to strip flesh from bone – not like their wild counterparts of years gone by. Rae growled faintly but, already, that very growl was growing lighter and lighter, as if it didn't quite sit right in his mouth anymore.

And that was okay. Especially as his crotch bubbled and changed, the skin and flesh there tugging taut, though he still had a small, neat tuck of a sheath. Daringly, Rae pulled down his underwear to his thighs, though only enough so that he could see what was between his legs, his cock emerging from his sheath in his arousal while his tail slicked all the way down into something more akin to the feline persuasion.

A house cat. Just a house cat. And yet he would be so much more than that too, becoming a silver tabby, the structure of his face shifting as his muzzle tickled and itched. He had a flatter face as a cat, with a shorter snout, though it didn't feel like that extra bone and flesh was really going anywhere, not leaving him, simply finding a new home on his face. His cheeks filled out softly, as if there was a permanent smile there, and longer whiskers grew, bright and white.

He had one paw on his growing, swelling cock, but the other trembled up to his face, allowing his fingers to brush those whiskers, surprised by just how sensitive the immediate feedback was from them. He could feel through them, though he had not used the shorter, stubbier ones on his canine snout as much as he felt he could as a cat anthro instead.

Yet who would know for just how long his transformation would last? Ah, his friend who had recommended the potion to him had not told him that much, though, at least, he had known it would be safe – and that was more than enough for Rae to want to take a softer break from reality.

In the body of another, he really could shrug off the shackles of everything else, grunting lightly. His ears twitched, drawing into wider bases, though they only had to thin down a little, no longer carrying hair on them that was as heavy as before. His tail felt strange, so much more flexible, though Rae didn't seem to be able to control it and flick it back and forth, not fully, not as easily as he had done. Well, a canine tail, not like the one that he had had only a few moments ago, simply did not have the same flexibility to it…

All those little muscles… They were not something that one thought about except when taking on the pleasure of transformation, in how it flowed over and through, a shroud that one would gladly embody. Everything had to be taken into account but, thankfully for Rae, that was not something that the transforming – feline rather than canine – had to consider. The potion took care of that for him but learning how to use his new body, even with the lighter, denser muscle of his thighs and arms drawing into easy focus in transformation, well… That was all up to Rae.

He didn't have to think about anything else, not as his shaft throbbed in his grasp. It changed slowly, tempting him to lock right down into the moment as if nothing else existed. He did not grow a knot at the base, even if that would only have inflated at the point of orgasm, but the length was no longer smooth either, not as he would have expected, but rising with little bumps, tiny nodules.

He would never grow true spines, like felines with feral ways, but there was a remnant of them there in the thick, fat barbs. They would have stimulated a sex partner, if he had not been alone at that time, but would not have hurt. Still, they seemed like they were designed to catch and pull in just the right way and he cautiously explored them, licking his lips.

"Mmm… Oh!"

Oh, that was *sensitive*! His finger had caught a barb, almost pulling it to the side, though there was not really any room between the "barb" and the shaft of his cock to catch, not when it came to something as thick as a finger. But it gave him something to play with, testing out just how he could pump his paw slowly up and down the length of his shaft, gripping the base. It even felt a little firmer, his balls a little plumper, his breath hitching a little more quickly in his throat.

But he couldn't stop, wouldn't stop, grunting and shaking his head, shoulders rounding even as he slumped backwards. Nothing made sense, sitting on his tail, one sensation clumsily crashing into the next, need and desire clouding his senses. Pre-cum dribbled lustfully down his cock, though it was not something he could hold back from, not in the slightest, not when his need was as great as it was.

He moaned lowly, trying to be quiet even when he didn't have to be such. He just had to allow it, had to have the moment, had to let the warmth flow through him, his toes curling.

Oh, his feet… He hadn't thought of how much his hind paws were going to change but a canine's paws were not the same as those of a feline's, becoming lighter, softer, smaller, more delicate. They were designed to be precise, though he had thought that he had quite a bit of stability in canine paws too. The pads were a little thinner and he shifted them on the thin carpet under his feet, allowing his mind to wander for a moment in sensation.

But his paw… It had to keep moving, lust rising, pushing through him, making him grunt and groan and rock his hips, a full feline anthro by that point. No one would have recognised him as Rae, though it would end up being the first time that Rae had orgasmed as a cat – yet not the last.

It was that which allowed him to clasp his paw around his cock more firmly, exploring and forcing himself on to those devious delights of pleasure. The bed bowed under him, his weight shifting, though Rae did not realise that he was curling forward a little, his paw working furiously, even sweeping down to brush over his balls, feeling the weight of them. It always returned swiftly to his cock, however, gripping and rubbing up and down, cautious of the barbs – yet not too worried anymore. They weren't going to catch on his paw and he could take all the pleasure that he wanted, pre-cum drooling from the head of his cock, his paw working furiously, pleasure burning.

It had to reach a peak, a burning crescendo, though Rae was barely even aware of the low, long groan rising from deep within his chest, as if it had only been waiting for a chance to be set free. He wanted it, needed it, craved it, panted heavily for it, though he could only snatch in what breaths that he could as orgasm roared through him.

He shook his head, strain at the base of his neck, though he was right where he needed to be, cum spurting from his cock in thick, drooling ropes, though they didn't need to go anywhere, no, nowhere at all. It was just in the pleasure of the moment, heat curling, pooling in the pit of his stomach. He moaned breathlessly, though not even Rae himself could be sure of just how far his cry went, if he even raised his voice at all.

With cum dribbling over his paw, he settled into his transformation, still unsure of how long it was going to last, though he didn't care. There would be many more orgasms like that as he ran his paws over a new body, exploring fur that was finer than his, the curves of muscles that did not hold a canine's thickness in them. There was no need to limit anything, of course, when it came to self-pleasure and the heady rise of it, a little bit sweaty as he panted, coming down from his high.

In feline transformation, Rae still had so much to uncover…

It was a good thing, for him, that the potion was going to last a good few hours yet!

# Call of the Wild

Jason sighed, standing on the edge of the cliff, his bare toes curled into the rock. Well, as much as it was possible, his feet a little on the straight side, grit digging into the underside of his bare feet, though he was still wearing thick trousers, the kind that came with a heavier, tougher fabric that was often worn for hiking.

He wasn't much of a hiker, however… No. No one looking at him, light and admittedly scrawny, would have considered him to be that kind of person. His hair was a little on the long side, as he hadn't had the chance to go have it trimmed in a while – or more so that it wasn't exactly his favourite place to head off to, never liking the buzz and the vibe of the men's barbershop.

"Hm…"

The Welsh mountains stretched out before him, though it was a grey sort of day. The sort of day, in fact, where they may have advised walkers and hikers to stay out of the mountains, for their own safety. There had been a storm warning out in the morning and the air had that strangely heavy, dull quality to it that seemed to come with a distinct sense of foreboding. There was a reason, after all, that it was called the "calm" before the storm.

Yet he was not there for a simple reason, no. Jason's lips parted softly, looking down the slopes, though the cliff would not have sent him tumbling down a sheer drop if he had taken a tumble over the edge, no. It spilt down into a rough scree of loose rock, though it came with an increment to the decline that suggested he would have been able to dig his fingers in and slow his fall, if it had come to that.

But there was a pull in Jason and he shifted his feet anxiously, waiting, watching. It was not for him to instigate the change – and yet it was coming one way or the other. He knew it in his gut, in the tug of his soul, as it pulled up inside him, drawing up and up and up. It was as if something was churning inside him, something that was not a physical part of him, but it was meant to be there too. It was only just making itself known to him.

"Please…"

Jason had been waiting for so long for the change. For the transformation. For the shift that would finally allow him to step into the ranks of his brethren. They were there with him, in spirit, but the first change had to come alone.

His time, as a shifter… It had finally *come*.

There was no ceremony to the transformation beginning, only a sense of something jolting inside him. No one watching Jason would ever have realised that something was happening to him as he stared adoringly down the range of the rich, green Welsh mountains, the craggy peaks touching the clouds. But he knew and that was all that the moment needed to be.

A private one, just for him, a moment that would, not even for Jason, not ever be replicated.

He shook his head, rolling his shoulders back, his clothes suddenly feeling tight and restrictive, as if his T-shirt was pulling taut across his chest. The neckline was too close to his neck and he grunted thickly in the back of his throat as he tugged at and fussed with it, shifting his weight, fingers curling and uncurling.

"Come on…"

Yet there was no amount of urging that he could do for the change to come, wanting so very desperately to join the ranks of the shifters, those that could transform, at will, between one animal and another. Whether they were anthro or some kind of animal that people were more familiar with, however, was another question entirely — and a shapeshifter would never know just what their animal was until their first change.

The call of the wild had come and it was time for him to pant and to heave, grunting as he tipped forward. It felt right to stretch his arms out, his fingers twitching, as if even that tiny part of his body was out of his control. His heartbeat fluttered. Since when had he not even been able to curl or clench his fingers?

Oh, that had been a long time, a very long time indeed, though Jason had to let it come, bit by bit, his back stiff, feeling like the entire upper section of his back was seized up.

"Unff…"

The wind swirled around him, picking up, lifting his T-shirt over his lower back as he dropped to all fours, groaning long and low. It hurt, pressure pushing up within him, snarling and snapping, his flesh rippling and bubbling.

"Unff… No… Something…"

He was trying to get words out even when Jason didn't even honestly know what it was he was trying to say. Tiny sensations became heightened, from the digging in of small stones into his palms to how heavy his body was and hard the rocky plateau, where he had been standing, was under his knees. It was not comfortable and it was never meant to be comfortable, not as his spine ached and ached, the sensation of it *stretching* drawing through him.

It was as if his body, or at the very least his spine, had become an elastic band, soft and pliable, malleable to a cause that was so very much larger than what he had anticipated. He panted heavily, his mouth thick and heavy with saliva, though he couldn't close his mouth enough to stop the light drool from slipping by his lips.

"Eugh…"

Jason shuddered, his trousers tight around his hips. That was the first part of his body that felt like it was going to burst free of the constraints of his clothes, his backside swelling, though it was with muscle and not fat. He panted, trying and failing to lick his lips, his tongue slopping out of his mouth as it hung there, oddly limp and too long for any memory that he had of the light but damp appendage.

"Gnnngghhh…"

He tried to close his eyes, but everything strained, as if he was trying to bulge and pop out of his own skin. It was more than enough for Jason to grapple with every last little change pushing and pulling through him, pressing urgently in on his mind for some kind of attention – any attention. He couldn't think about everything all at once, not as something, most likely a tail, pushed from the base of his spine, his body swelling and growing, the pain of new muscles forming coming like a glowing burn.

But it was not true pain, no, not when his body was meant to be changed. Jason was lucky, in that sense, that he had been born with a shape-shifting gene, his mother and his father both shifters. They expected it from him, though they had hoped he would be a wolf or a canid of some kind, just like them.

It did not seem to be the case for Jason, however, not as his trousers split down the buttocks and between the legs, revealing his blue boxers beneath as he grunted and heaved. His underwear did not last much longer either as warmth consumed him, his skin prickling with heat and even tiny beads of sweat rolling down his skin. They pooled in the dip between his shoulder blades, though it felt quite as if the muscle all over his body was growing more and more defined, allowing those shifts and rises to capture increasing amounts of sweat.

And yet...it was changing too. All as that tail pushed from his spine, using the tear in his trousers to force its way out, writhing and wriggling. It itched something fierce, as if a thousand sharp nails were being raked down it at the same time, seeming to come out more and more and more from his body.

Longer, surely, than a canine's tail would be... Or even the tail of a wolf, like his father.

Jason sucked in a breath, which was more difficult than he expected to do so with such tightness around his lungs, as if there was no longer adequate space for his organs within the cage of his ribcage. His tail was longer, yes, like that of a reptile, and he snarled, pushing up on his legs, shifting up onto his toes.

It was a more comfortable position for him, the transforming man's thighs so thick that they too forced his clothes to split down the back of them, his body aching deeply. Yet with every throbbing pulse of sensation came another thrum of desire, a push to want to be in his true form, his real body, what had taken him right up into his mid-twenties to finally claim for his own.

"Mmmph... Yessssssth..."

He groaned, shaking his head, though tried to part his lips in a smile even then. His arms lengthened, the bones crunching and cracking, though it was more the memory of the sudden crunch that had him shuddering than the shifting and repositioning of his arms. Though he could see, at least, that they were not arms anymore, not as the skin and flesh flowed fluidly over his hands.

The fingers lengthened and the nails tightened down into long, hook-like claws, claws that could both grip and rend, claws that would be more than suitable for slicing through prey, if it ever came to that. He could hunt, yes, for he was a predator, and he let out a raspy, hissing sort of laugh as his hands became feet, no longer a biped but a quadruped, quite clearly.

Or getting there, at least. He heaved and panted, his shirt pulling under his arms, though it was something bulging up from his shoulder blades that tore through it. One moment the strain was there across his chest and the next it was relieved, the fabric hanging limply around his shoulders and chest, as a pair of wings slowly grew.

Jason battled with the notion, shaking his head, his tongue gaining a little more mobility. It slimmed down slightly, but what he noticed the most with it was the length, wriggling and twisting, a light fork present right at the tip. It slopped against his teeth as they itched, a deep, pushing strain showing just how they were growing from his jaw, sharper, pointier... They didn't need to hold molars in there anymore. He tried to experimentally sweep his tongue around his mouth, but it didn't quite feel like there were incisors in there anymore either, trying to flick his tail back and forth. The heavy weight of it dragged his back end to the side, however, putting him off-balance, grunting, groaning, doing no more than bearing through the weight of the changes overpowering his body.

Yet his skin... It was not as it had been, not as it grew rougher and he shook himself, trying to get the shreds of his clothes off. Patches of scales erupted over his body, randomly, his skin first turning a darker shade, a rich red that caught the eye and made him want to shelter in it, so glorious was the development. An orange line, sharp and striking, clawed down his side as Jason groaned and stretched his back legs out a little, testing how his natural stance would lie, the weight of his tail somehow managing to balance him. That would be just another thing to get used to, for it was not as if he was used to standing and moving on four legs rather than two.

Let alone flying with both wings and a tail…

That would be something for later, however, as he grunted and licked his lips, gaining increasing control over his body. The itching and prickling of his scales, however, was difficult to bear through, his head feeling bigger and heavier as his jaw expanded, his skull aching deeply with the extension of his jaw.

"Mmph…"

He could barely talk and moving was hard, feeling weighed down and even more a part of the ground under his feet than he ever had felt before. He didn't know what to think, even though he knew what he was becoming, just who and what he was transforming into. Soon, his heart would soar as high as his wings could ever carry him, though that was something for Jason to come to imagine later.

In the moment, his scales prickled and bit into his body, becoming a part of his flesh, skin transforming. They spread more and more, covering his nakedness, yet the transforming dragon could not deny the clawing, unbridled heat that was simmering deep within the pit of his stomach.

He needed…something. The drake hissed and tried to lick his lips, even though he didn't quite have full control over his body yet, his muzzle scaled, nostrils slipping down into neat little slits, though they would be more than capable of drawing enough air into his lungs. The pressure on the back of his head and his neck, along the line of his spine, was immense, but it eased as his neck fleshed out with muscle. A dragon, after all, did not have a short, stubby neck, not like a human. No, they were beastly and elegant, both at the same time, and he was so much more than the man that he had been, sucking in breath after breath, finally managing to lick his lips as the heat of his body, and his scales, evaporated away every last drop of sweat.

It was not meant to be there, after all, not as a dragon. Dragons did not sweat and needed other means, such as spreading their wings, using the air and opening their maws widely, to cool down, though his body had warmed through the course of the transformation. Jason grunted and clenched his jaw, hard, trying to roll his shoulders back as he found his wings went along with them.

His transformation was at a stage where he was rendered more dragon than human, though there were still a few bare patches of skin remaining. As his skull ached deeply with horns growing, just two, one on either side of his head, his hair fell away, drifting and wisping as if it had never truly been a part of his body in the first place. Jason grunted, his head and neck set a little more comfortably again as he faced forward, extended out like that of a quadruped rather than still trying to hold onto a bipedal form.

No… It was better like that, so much better. He may not have been a serpent, but he shed one skin for another as the leathery skin of his wings stretched out and out and out, spreading between the spines of his wings. Energy had to come from somewhere to transform such a body, however, and he swayed lightly, dizzy from the mental and physical exertion that had come from it. And yet everything would ease in time, even if Jason would, later, find he was not able to fly home to see his family and the other shifters, his body needing to first recover.

His body, after all, was not fully transformed. Without a scrap of pale skin left, scales covered his body completely, his tail growing into a blade-like weapon, made of horn, at the end. It weighed him down, but the muscling there soon caught up, layering his tail and his glutes so that he could better balance with his tail, even if it would take time to fully use it as self-defence and hunting. Under his belly, close to the join of his body to his legs, where his crotch would have been before, his shaft hung, though it was soft…too soft. It did not need to be there on his body, not like that, not as it dangled and softly sucked back into his body.

"Mmm…"

Jason groaned and shook his head, tongue hanging out. Oh, that was a good feeling, pressure around his shaft, even as his cock was tucked away, rather than growing. He grunted and stomped, his toes curling and nails growing into hind claws on the backs too, but he was thinking about other things. Even as his back grew a light dip in it, rising to the sensually powerful curve of his hindquarters, his attention was on the slit that his cock had softened into. His balls melted inside him, but there was no sense of loss at all, not as the dragon grunted and rolled his eyes, trying his best to make sense of his body.

He had not heard of shifters struggling with arousal during transformation before, though perhaps it was something to do with them being embarrassed about it. They could be a very private sort and that was exactly why shapeshifters more often than not stuck to their community and the like, everyone there brushing up against everyone else. But they did not too often go into detail on their first changes, experiencing it all as a very private event indeed.

And that was okay too, as long as they were able to take it for themselves, even though his shaft throbbed and ached, pressing urgently back out against the edge of the slit that had formed. It needed to come out, his internally held testes aching and churning, something pushing inside him, though it was not a change. No... It was merely arousal, merely desire, something that had to come through in pulse after pulse, a new shaft emerging.

No longer would he have the smooth-skinned human shaft, no... No, that would not be for Jason, not as he stood there, on all fours, a feral beast, a dragon worthy of the name as he grew larger and larger, his entire body trying to catch up all at once. Muscle swelled and his bones crunched as they were forced to lengthen, growing larger than a draft horse and bigger still.

Dragons were not small, after all, and neither was his cock as it dripped clear pre-cum, the length dark-skinned in a rich ruby and slowly fleshing out in knobs and ridges. There didn't seem to be any special design to it that the eye could follow, but the ridges were more than designed for the pleasure of a partner, even though they seemed to spiral anxiously, as if they were clinging to his shaft. The knobs and spike-like nodules ringed the head, which tapered to a rounded point, and he growled, rolling his hips forward, his fully formed wings spreading wide as he panted heavily through an open maw.

"Mmmm..."

He would try out his new vocal cords later, for arousal trembled through him, fully a dragon even though he was still growing, swelling, the rock crunching under him as his weight affected his stance. In the end, Jason would get to the size of a bungalow, a single-storey home, but the process of arousal was something else.

He felt it all, the trembling power of his transformation, how his need ached through his body so very deeply, making him want to hump and grind and rock his hips. It was carnal and it was feral and it was everything that Jason had never even known, his cock drooling. He didn't need to grip it with a hand or anything that could ever be as crude, though he could lean into it, how flowing, throbbing power rose within him.

And it was that which sent sensation to his cock, rendering him so over-sensitive that even the lick and the brush of air moving by his massive member made him want to hump and thrust, hissing out ardently through his teeth. The dragon snarled, lips peeling back, though Jason couldn't quite decide on a single course of action at any given time, tail sweeping back and forth, lashing the air. Maybe that was one of the reasons why he had been chosen to transform, for the first time, in an open space, for he could have really done some serious damage to a house or even a forest if he had been in tighter confines.

Out there, however, as his body grew in proportion, up to the size of the largest of draft horses, huffing and puffing, he could do anything, be anything. And all the dragon had to relish in was the experience of his body filling up, how muscles thickened up, new matter formed from substances that had had no presence before. Only in magic, the sweeping, overriding magic of transformation that was the will of every shapeshifter, would the new form of his body be made.

His spines prickled to life down the line of his neck – and then his entire spine. The draconic shape was his, the weapon at the tip of his tail lighter while his body strained to encompass it, to be able to hold and wield it as he was meant to. Yet all was right with the world and his little part of it too, grunting and groaning, letting his cock throb and throb and throb with passionate need.

"Unff... Yes..."

The first words, as a dragon, slipped from his maw in lust, exactly as it should have been, and his tongue slapped out wetly against the side of his muzzle. Jason was too far gone to take full note of it, rolling his hips, humping and grinding. He didn't even have his eyes open anymore to take in the scope of the rolling hills and mountains spread out before him, concentrating only on sensation, his own passion, while his body grew and grew.

It would take Jason more than a little while to get a handle on the full scope of his transformed body but there was nothing there to hold him back, not as something pulled tighter and tighter between his legs. It had to have been contained in his internally held testes, where they were safely tucked away for more aerodynamic, as a dragon, purposes, though Jason did not care. Not in that moment, not as his massively thick, ridged cock pulsed and drooled, big globs of pre-cum slopping forth to splatter wetly on the ground. It marked his claws, even where it landed, yet the drake did not even notice, not as his tail swung and heat swelled, as if he was burning up from the inside out.

And maybe he was. Maybe that was the way of dragon shifters too, for they were not the kind of shifter that Jason had ever met before.

He would have to ask them, one day.

But not then. Not as orgasm swelled, a roaring bellow that coursed up from his gut, lips parted, snarling his delight to the mountain range before him. Yet all Jason's mind was focused on was the pulse and the throb of his achingly hard member, fully grown as a dragon and spending every drop of seed that his oversized body had.

His wings stretched out, shaking, trying to remain steady while he spread them out a little more, though Jason simply did not yet have control over that part of his body, not in full. It would come in time, all in good time, ropes of thick, sticky cream arcing from his cock as if the act of orgasm had become an art form. Transformation in itself was an art and something that only a shifter truly in control of themselves could achieve alone; yet another skill that Jason was going to have to work at, training a very particular kind of muscle in his body.

Yet the drake heaved, his great flanks shuddering for breath, feeling his cum leaving him, how it felt like it was all being squeezed from his body, stream after streaming rope of it. It had to come, of course, for it could not stay there, not as his head hung and he tilted it to the side. A light smile tugged at the corner of his lips, though he would take his time in getting used to those muscles too and all the facial expressions he would have to learn, all over again, as a dragon.

His orgasm… That was easier to lean into. Even though he would find ways to climax and to get himself off more easily, in time, the change itself would always end up being an orgasm-inducing event for the lusty dragon shifter.

And that was all it had to be. For one shapeshifter and all the others, finding passion in transformation and, of course, the experience of a new body.

# Taking a Change

Taylor sighed, leaning back with his arm across his eyes, shading his face from the sun. It was such a pain to be out in the sunshine with nothing to do, though the weekend preceding had been pretty okay, really. But the fact of the matter was that he had missed the last train, before the cancellations and strikes and all that, back from the seaside town, so he was stuck there for longer.

"Ugh..."

And there was nothing going on there either. The day was so quiet that there simply didn't seem to be anything at all to occupy his time, most of the places that he would hang out at, if he was on his own, closed for a bank holiday day. Even then, a lot of places would more often than not be open on those days – but it was a special day and a quiet town down on the coast. They liked to take time off whenever it was offered to them and, frankly, he didn't blame them one bit for that.

When his train was cancelled, however, and he was just waiting for the little hotel to allow him in for the evening, not expecting check-in until at least four in the afternoon, he had to stay there. At least it was nicer on the beach when it was quiet, a pier down to his left, though he had walked down a considerable way already, just to make sure he wasn't around anyone. His friends would have said that he was a guy who liked his privacy and Taylor was more than a little "social'd out" after spending time with friends.

The white sand sifting through his fingers, warmed by the first touches of the summer sun, was nice, however, the heat playing across his face. There was just the problem of not really wanting to be there, of preparing himself for the travel home and then understanding, suddenly, he couldn't head back when he'd planned.

Disruptions to anything, well... To him, they were the worst.

He rolled his eyes, though they were already mostly closed, an old beach towel under him. At least the sand was pretty white and nice, the kind that was made from crushed shells and the like, though he had seen plenty of beaches. If only his friend, Liam, had not had things to do that day, away, that meant that he couldn't just pop back there.

Liam, however, had given him a bag of small coins... What was all that about?

"Probably something freaky... Liam... Huh..."

Taylor would have scoffed, but, at the very least, it was something to do when he was stuck for, well, anything else to consider. His mind drifted, flipping back and forth, still lying on the blanket while he dug around in his pocket, hearing the bag of coins jingle as they clanked and jangled against one another. Even that sound grated on his ears and, subconsciously, he shuddered away from it.

Curious and, frankly, bored out of his own mind, he fished the small bag of coins, in a velvety pouch (though he was sure it was not velvet), that his friend had given him.

"Take one to start a change," he said, reading aloud from the embroidered writing on the outside. "Hm..."

The beach was quiet but, knowing his friend, well... Hah! It probably wasn't going to be anything in the pouch or the coins that he should have been doing in public.

He glanced back and forth, nipping at the inside of his lower lip, where his lip connected to his cheek. Did he dare? Oh, it was ridiculous, really...but the sex toy industry had been doing some freaky things lately, even if they were only temporary. It was probably a good thing that it was only temporary…

Taylor didn't know what was happening, but that was okay. Or, more accurately, he didn't know what *would* happen when he flipped one of the golden-tone coins in the air, the coating rubbing off on his hand. He pursed his lips, the towel rumpling under him where he was lying, though something pushed within him, jolting in the middle of his stomach as if it was trying to get out of him.

"Ugh… Oh, that feels kinda…"

He closed his hand around the coin, his head light, a more relaxed smile playing across his lips. Down there, he was a stranger to everyone around him, though there was something of a risk, a tantalising risk, in letting what was going to happen *happen* right there, out in public. As if he had nothing else in his mind, a being with no further consequences.

His stomach trembled, churning, grumbling. Taylor hoped, if only for a moment, that it was not going to be anything to do with inflation; he didn't quite fancy transforming into a beach ball or big dragon on the beach, though he had known that some of his friends had tried those transformation tricks. Apparently, when they were non-sexual, the tokens that people could pick up for them were great fun at parties.

Yet it was not as if he was going to take part in his own transformation as he settled there, his breath hitching a bit, breathing just a little bit more swiftly before. Yet he was acutely aware of every last tiny bit of his body, from the curl of his toes to the shaped pressure of the hard sand under his back, how it moulded to the shape of his body. Taylor tried to lick his lips, though they felt strange… As if they had become thicker and heavier than before.

"Agh… Damnnnneet…"

And he couldn't talk either. If he wasn't sure that everything would come out as a garbled mess, he would have tried to say more, but he clamped his mouth shut for the moment. With his heart pounding more swiftly again, something jolted and leapt within him – higher up that time. It was in his chest and not his stomach, though he twitched and wriggled his fingers, curling them into the blanket, though a few grains of sand remained obstinately clinging to the palms of his hands.

It soaked into him, his legs kicked out before him, though Taylor would later consider himself quite lucky he had worn shorts that day. Or, more specifically, shorts that he didn't care about all that much.

So…it wouldn't matter all that much when they ripped.

His legs… There was something "wrong" with his legs, feeling like they were sticking together. He grunted, shifting his weight back and forth, holding his hands out before him – though his hands changing colour to a light yellow should not have been his focus. It was one of the easiest parts of his body, however, for him to focus on, turning them over, watching with wide eyes and strained breath, tight in his throat, as his nails disappeared.

It was like…they just melted away. Something on his fingers softened and he was left with a spreading mass of scale-like skin, though it reminded him of something else too. The yellow spread, splashed through with darker yellow lines – like markings?

"Huh, it isss a transssform… Huh? Transsssformat… What isss thisss?"

His tongue seemed too thick in his mouth, slipping back and forth, his lips longer, his face pushing out. Taylor tried to gulp but his tongue didn't know where to go, his teeth growing slimmer and thinner.

There were fewer of them in his mouth, but he didn't feel at all like anything was shrinking, so it couldn't have been that bad of a transformation. Even then, it was something he liked, though, frankly, he hadn't been able to afford the transformation tokens when he'd spotted them in the shops before.

Liam, on the other hand, was rather flush with cash. Whether it was a prank or a gesture of goodwill, Taylor could not help but grin as widely as he was able, two of his teeth near the front of his mouth growing larger and longer than the others, hooking down sharply.

*I think I know…*

But Taylor did not have to fully understand what was happening to him, as long as he was on board with it. That was all that mattered, truly, that he was in agreement with it, for he'd heard that transformation tokens didn't even work if it was not something that someone wanted. A failsafe of some kind…

He didn't care. Not as he let out another hissing moan and let his mind go to his legs, where they felt like they were squeezing in against one another. As if his skin was sticky with sweat, they peeled in against each other, from the top down, forcing his shorts to strain tighter and tighter across the crotch until they ripped through. Heat raced to his cheeks, brightening hot, flushed patches on his neck too, though there was no one there, even though he was briefly exposed.

Taylor hissed, trying to control his tongue, which seemed to constantly want to slop awkwardly out of his mouth as his face extended forward, eyes positioned forward still – which was a relief. It didn't seem like the top half of his body was changing too much, though the same could not be said of his legs, not as they fused. His feet softened as he looked tentatively down at himself, heart pounding, cock semi-hard and thick with arousal, bits of him exposed that should not have been. However, it was not as if it could have been said to be a public beach, not really, when it was deserted.

Still, he allowed the transformation to progress, wrapping around him as he if he was shedding his skin, replacing one hide with another. Taylor huffed a grunt as his nose flattened out, smoothing down to the front of his face, though it was almost as if his entire face was a nose, becoming a snout and giving him that impression, at least for the moment.

"Mmmph!"

His jaws… There was something there, a sense of looseness – and strength at the same time. Experimentally, even as they changed, he opened and closed his mouth, feeling how the base of his mouth flattened out, leaving a channel for his tongue. His tongue instinctively seemed to not want to go too close to his teeth, in particular those big, hooked ones, the ones that reminded him of fangs.

*Oh!*

That made sense, Taylor giving a delicious little shiver as he more keenly looked down at the softening, melding blob of his legs. That looked more like a single tail, clad in that leathery, scaley skin, than anything else, his feet finally smoothing out all the way into a rounded, tapered tip to said tail.

And then he understood, laughing aloud, even though it came out in a hissing rasp that would not have had any place on human lips. His tail wriggled back and forth limply, loosely, and it was a strange feeling indeed to make sense of the bones in his legs becoming no more than an extension of his spine. It suctioned down, clicking and crunching, though the sensations popping through him were, thankfully, only mildly uncomfortable.

Uncomfortable, awkward transformations… Well, those were not something he had honestly ever been interested in.

But to be there, experiencing it all for the first time… That was something to *relish*! He groaned open-mouthed, letting his tongue slip out, careful of the fangs. For a naga could be venomous too and he didn't want to harm himself accidentally, even though it was more likely everything would be okay for a transformation like that.

His legs swelled – well, no, not his legs, but his tail. It was a tail despite it being very difficult to think of a part of his body like that, heartbeat racing and lust finally catching up with him. Taylor shook his head slowly, pushing himself up with his arms, fingers sinking into the sand where it had not compacted down, his shoulders feeling a bit bigger, more rounded out with muscle than before.

But that was something that he was not all that interested in, no. How could he concern himself with his body growing more powerful, in moderation, when he had a *tail*? That surely overruled all else! He tried to slide it back and forth, to work out the changing, growing muscles down the length of it, though everything felt thick and heavy, as if it was something weighing him down.

"Unff…"

Taylor grunted, parting his lips and letting his tongue rest inside, a pale yellow-white appendage that he only caught a quick glimpse of. His head was not settling but it could not remain purely in the raw shape of a human skull, his eyes set forward, like those of a predator, tongue flickering in and out, in and out, more comfortably. If he didn't think about it too much, it looked like instinct took over, letting him be more serpentine, even though a naga, with the top half of a humanoid and the bottle half of a snake, was not fully a snake.

No. He was different. And he could languish in that, the twisting push and pull of his tail curling and sweeping back and forth, even if it was only a few inches from one side to the other, the weight of his body feeling just a little less solid when there was muscle and strength to come too. He was not fully in tune with snake anatomy, but he knew there were ligaments and fascia, everything that connected a body and allowed it to work properly, to come into place too.

His face, however, settled into a snake-like shape with a long jaw and narrow nostrils, a more tapered snout than Taylor might have been expecting. Yet what was unprecedented, once he'd realised just what he was transforming into, was the swell of extra leathery skin around his face. He did not quite trust himself to move his hands from the ground, where he was still balancing and bracing himself, but that was okay. He could still take it all in, feeling the skin stretch out from the back of his head, drawing up into a smooth, cobra-like hood.

"Huh…"

He shook his head, his skin cooling, though even that came with a new weight to it, kind of as if he was wearing a hat. Yet it was a hat that was a part of him, something that could be folded in a little or spread out in a dominating, threatening posture. Of course, cobras were not typically aggressive and everything they did that may have been considered intimidating was purely to get other creatures to leave them alone, but perhaps that was different for a naga. Maybe he could be confident in leaving his hood open, splayed out proudly with streaks of darker yellow markings to cut through the fainter shades of his scales? There were even richer markings too, an orangey kind of brown, as if they were drawn deliberately, painted on his form purely to draw attention to them.

Taylor tried to smile, but the most that he seemed able to do was part his lips, for they did not twitch easily up at the corners anymore. His fangs hooked down nicely without interfering with either his lips or his jaw, the tip of his tail twitching, though sitting up like that was not quite a natural position either. The hood spread as much as he was able to flare it out, the tug of muscles at the base of it controlling it, though he would have to splay it out again soon when he lost that tiny bit of control.

"Sssso…"

Every word came with a hiss and that was what got Taylor to chuckle softly. He wouldn't have normally been as vocal as he was being in that moment, his tail thickening up more and more, easily as long as his torso was and still growing.

"Sssso much tail… Why'sss there ssso much?"

He hissed as he spoke, though tried to control it with a bubble of mirth in the centre of his chest. It was just – fun! And could it just be fun? The sun was still shining down with barely any fluffy clouds in the sky, even if he was feeling a little more chilled than before. Could snakes like him, in a transformed form, need to bask in the sun too?

His tail elongated but what was left of his cock retreated too into a neat slit at the base of his belly – or where he presumed his crotch would have been before. It was still there, of course, and he exhaled briefly, glad that a sense of loss had not come through at the same time. That could have been very uncomfortable, at least for him, even if he barely understood what was going on in terms of how his anatomy was changing. Taylor would certainly be reading up on it later on, however, just to make sure he was clued up on as many little details about what had happened to him as possible…

In the moment, however, it was simply too intoxicating to let his changes settle over him, rising to balance haphazardly, wobbling back and forth as if his tail was made of very firm jelly. His fingers traced around that slit, marvelling at how it appeared as if that was how his body had always been, not a glitch or a defect at all to be seen.

"Amazzzing…"

Huh, so he even wanted to drag out his "z's" in a hiss. That was funny, kind of, but the slit at the base of his belly parted softly at the touch of his fingers. Although he was still getting used to his body, the weight of it, how he made a curved indent in the sand, the towel tangled down there somewhere, arousal taking the lead above all else.

"Mmmm…"

He moaned, more deeply than he would have before, but his heart leapt and pounded, his transformation complete. It was hard to tell just how tall he was, but his tail was twice the length, at least, of his torso, long and thick, able to curl with muscle and undulate back and forth, for it was what was meant to sweep and push him across the ground. It would be nothing like legs, but it was fortunate too that his abdominal muscles, along with the muscles in his lower back, appeared to be stronger than before too. That allowed him to "stand" upright with his torso, wriggling his tail back and forth to cautiously nudge his body forward, testing the limits.

Yet other things rose to the forefront of his mind, his desire to explore his new body coming up against the needs of his body. His slit parted, allowing the tip of his cock out and yet…it was not the same as it had been when it had gone into his belly-slit. Taylor's heart leapt and his stomach churned, though it was with excitement and not fear, his scaled hide itching and tingling as if he was already prepared to shed his skin.

That, however, would not come to pass when he was in a naga form, not one but two cocks sliding from his slit. He groaned, rolling his "hips" forward, tail shuddering as he struggled to balance, getting better and better at it with every passing moment. It was simply difficult to think about anything else when his desire was as high as it was, a cautious hand grasping the two cocks, the hemipenes that swelled to attention, wanting everything that he had there to offer them.

And that was lust. Pleasure. Desire curling through, like the twist of a serpent's tail.

Taylor turned his head slowly from one side to the other, taking his time, as if he was sweeping the beach for any other people. The difference there was that he was doing it merely as a performative action, for Taylor knew that he didn't really have to hold back there. No one, after all, was ever going to recognise him as a naga, his features so very different to how they had been as a man.

His hemipenes throbbed and, even then, he knew what he had to do, the pale, pink flesh begging his attention as he slowly slid his hand up and down, feeling just how firm the flesh was, harder than his cock had been as a man. Maybe that was a feature of being a naga, but he found that he simply did not care. One thing that he *did* care about, however, was just how annoying his T-shirt was in that moment, feeling too tight around his shoulders, tugging up under the arms. It was still usable and wearable, though not to the extent, if he had been human, he would have felt comfortable wearing it out in public or for any significant length of time.

"Heh…" He hissed, tongue slapping out outside his mouth: something that he would have to get used to controlling over time. "Guessss I don't need thesssse anymore…"

He drew his T-shirt, however tight it already was, up and over his head, struggling to balance on his thick tail. There was plenty of muscle there, though he couldn't balance and steady himself yet, even if he would learn. He didn't yet know how long the transformation was going to last – but he most certainly going to have to get back in touch with his friend! It was not as if he could simply slither around the beach town until he randomly transformed back! And he would be naked then too!

That, however, in his current form, all on his own out there with the waves rolling softly onto the shore, was not entirely a bad thing. In fact, it was a very good thing as he more carefully licked his lips. That was more of a human action than a serpentine one, for snakes flickered out their tongues to taste the air, but it just hung there, a notion his body wanted to complete even if it was no longer needed.

There was so much more to understand… And he took his time. With his clothes bundled up into his arms, shredded shorts and underwear and all, he slithered up the beach into the dunes. He was fortunate that they even remained there, though it had to be to do with some kind of conservation, for which he was grateful. He could have done what he wanted right there out on the beach, frankly, but something in his new body and mind sought out a sun-warmed spot that was a little more secluded than before.

The snaking, serpentine motion of his body swept him across the sand and into the dunes, slithering down a light slope with the spill of lightly hissing sand coming along with him. Taylor did not need words, not as he rose to his full height in the soft seclusion of the dunes, tossing his clothes aside. The dunes there were not as big or as foreboding as others in other coastal parts of the country that he had seen before, though they were tall enough to hide him, or at least give him a little warning if he was going to be come upon in a hurry.

And the throbbing pulse of his hemipenes drove him on, taking one in each hand, marvelling at them.

"Sssuch a handful…"

It was strange to have a bigger cock – and not only one of them but two. Every beat of his heart forced blood into them, the tissue forced swelling to display itself proudly, the cocks tapered lightly, though they didn't both seem to curve in the same direction. It was very gentle curve, however, and one that allowed them to rest, if he released them from the grip of his hand, ever so gently against one another.

"Mmmmm…"

The depth of the groan surprised even Taylor, a lusty reverberation pulling up from deep within him, grunting, groaning, panting very faintly through parted lips. It didn't feel like his breath was washing over his tongue, even then, but he tried to let everything come as it was meant to, blinking slowly, his slim tongue flickering lustfully in and out of his mouth.

It definitely took two hands on his cocks to please himself, at least like that. But he had two hands, even as a naga, and that was more than okay with Taylor, pumping slowly but surely up and down the length of both dicks. There was a swell in the bottom third, a light bulge that took up a few inches of the length, and he played his fingers over it, giving it a testing squeeze.

After being in his belly-slit, both of his shafts had a lightly sticky, "glommy" feel to them, as if there was some manner of lubrication in there that helped them ease from his slit and remain ready to function. Or maybe it was pre-cum? Either way, more pre-cum beaded at the tip of both cocks, though not evenly, betraying him as far more than "just" a snake.

A snake would not have presented pre-cum like that, but that was all well and good with him, taking on a body that was fantasy, that was designed, at that time, purely for fetish and no more than that. Sometimes, things did not have to be any more than exactly what they were and there was a big part of Taylor that liked that.

People were so insistent on applying greater, deeper meanings to things that did not have to be anything more than what they were, something that he had seen time after time again. But they could be as they were in sensation only, if he wanted that too. He could truly lock down and into the feeling of his hand closing around his cock, how it slid up and down, forcing the fingers to part a little more widely around the bulge.

"Mmmm... Yesssss..."

There... Yes, it was there he could lose himself. He would be found again afterwards, of course, but there was no need for him to worry about anything, not as he licked his lips, controlling his tongue a little better than he had before, flickering it in and out, in and out. Although his light-coloured tongue gleamed as it moved over his lips, there was by no means an excess of saliva in his mouth, merely just a feature of the slick, smooth appendage, all in how it caught the light.

His cocks throbbed. That in itself wasn't unusual, but it was in how they dripped and drooled, thick dollops of nearly clear pre-cum sliding down his lengths. It dropped over his fingers, marking them even as he used his own drooling pre-cum to lubricate his cocks, working his hands in opposite strokes. When one hand went up, the other went down, ensuring that he was never devoid of pleasure that came in aching pulses, desire curling up into the pit of his stomach.

He hissed, twisting his tail back and forth, knowing what he was doing and yet unable to stop. The day was well in progress and a ray of sunshine cast over him through a break in the light, fluffy clouds, an ocean breeze tickling his snakeskin, the hood around his head twitching faintly as if it was trying to fold back in. One moment crossed the one that came before it, bungled and tangled. Yet he didn't pause.

There was no need to, though he tried to slow the pull of his thoughts, just how frantic they were as they pressed on through his mind, aching as if he was about to lose control of his body. His tongue lashed out in a slap against the side of his snout, hissing rampantly, twisting and curling, struggling between lust and the fairly basic need of balance. He didn't want to slump into the sand, even though it would have sifted off his snakeskin either way, wanting more than anything else to be up and present for that moment of penultimate orgasm.

It rose tenaciously, like a snake's head rising from the basket of a snake charmer, even if Taylor was not a serpent to be charmed in the slightest. He panted heavily, chest shuddering with breath, his glowing, yellow skin on full display, from head to toe, though he did not feel naked at all. Even with his hemipenes out, throbbing and drooling, more and more pre-cum slopping from him as his need flared, too thick and too fast to even consider being controlled.

"Unff… Yesss… It'sss…coming!"

He threw his head back, letting his tongue lash, his tail slapping the ground, hiss after hiss blurring his speech. Yet the naga didn't need to be clear, he didn't need to enunciate, not as orgasm took him. Thick, hot, heady ropes of cum poured lustfully from his cock, spurt after spurt, coming as if they were trying to force themselves up as deeply as possible into a partner. Yet he was there alone and perhaps he would have to take that kind of passion with a partner at another time, seeing just how hard he could pound someone with his hemipenes, in a transformed body, for mutual lust and pleasure.

That was something for another time, however, and he would have to take everything that he was given splattering the sand with his seed where it lay in dark ropes, lightly soaking into the sand to mark where it hit. He licked his lips breathlessly, coming down slowly from his orgasm, yet nothing could take the prickling, warming heat of climax from his body, how he felt warmed through even though, in that body, he was cold-blooded. His tail shifted, adjusting the weight of him in the sand, feeling the presence of his body more securely and heavily than ever.

"Mmm…"

He breathed out, laughing faintly, though even that came with a rasping hiss.

Such a moment… And a moment that he would seek to replicate as he went through every last one of the transformation tokens Liam had, very kindly, gifted him. He was, however, going to have to find a new pair of shorts – underwear too, if he could get his hands on any – from a back garden or even an open shop, if he dared go in with the shreds of his current pair of ruined shorts hanging from him. There had to be a way to clip them together, temporarily, but he would concern himself with that when he changed back to a man.

For the moment, his hands slid to the base of his dicks and *squeezed*.

As a naga, there was more *pleasssure* in taking a change still to be gleaned for his own…

# Taking Flight

Mack smirked, the wingless dragon anthro sitting with his legs dangling over the edge of a ledge, looking down on the mountain range below him. A mist of light rain hung in the air and someone else may have considered the day to be dull and grey, clouds scudding across the sky as the wind chased them along their way.

He adored being away from the city, relaxing in brighter, greener landscapes. Everything in the city was so manufactured, anthros living lives that had been set out for them in weird and wonderful ways. His scales were so smooth, lying flat against his body, that there was hardly any definition at all between them, though his green hide did sparkle in the sunshine, highlighting the difference shades across them, coming from different angles. A narrow line of horn-like spikes protruded from Mack's cheekbones, pointing back towards his neck, along with the typical two horns, lightly curved upward. A line of spines running down his back to the triangular tip of his tail completed his look, a typical dragon.

The only problem for Mack was…he could not fly. He had been born without wings, just like some dragons, and, well…he had always wanted to. Even when he had been young, he had spent playtime after playtime running around pretending that he was a hawk or some other bird of prey, spreading his arms wide in lieu of wings. Of course, he had been teased for that, because kids would find any reason possible to tease someone, but Mack was fortunate enough that it had not lingered.

A flightless dragon… Others had wings and were not able to fly, while others had been born with a hollow bone structure and air sacs within their bodies to gift them that additional buoyancy.

Luckily for the dragon, there were potions that could fix that, those days. That was helpful, so very much so – but Mack would never have taken his particular challenge on in a way that was boring and conventional, oh no.

Grinning, he pulled the small potion bottle – named like it was out of a fantasy game, so funny – out of his pocket and dragged the cork stopper out with his teeth. It was just a trial, a test for him to see how things went, and the dragon really should have had someone there with him to make sure that he'd be okay. Yet Mack had wanted to ensure that he had both the time and the privacy to enjoy his new wings, drinking the entire potion down in a couple of gulps, his throat working furiously.

"Ah…"

The wind picked up a little, licking at his scales. Even though Mack was just in a T-shirt, he licked his lips and leaned back, not chilled in the slightest. He did prefer basking in the sunshine to warm up, though the chillier weather was a welcome relief too, rather than constantly wiping himself down with cooler water in an effort to reduce his body temperature in the summer months.

*I wonder how quickly this is meant to work?*

The dragon didn't have to worry for too much longer, however, as he flexed his fingers, his scales itching oddly. He'd worn light cotton trousers, not really suited for hiking up into the mountains, and a loose T-shirt for his transformation. The drake didn't even know how much he was going to change, so he'd tried to be prepared. If he headed back down, after the temporary transformation, with his shirt a bit shredded though, that probably wouldn't be such a bad thing.

"Mmm…"

Mack hummed softly to himself as he swung his tail back and forth, not at all concerned by the height he was at, his legs kicking in the open air. He parted his jaw, teeth aching, though the uncomfortable sensations were not worrisome to him in the slightest, for it was all part of shedding one skin for another.

"Unff..."

Still, he couldn't stop himself from letting out a grunt as he shifted his weight, pressing back a little more as he leaned back on his hands. His head felt strange, as if there was an extra weight there that had not been present before, tipping his head to the side, his horns too large and cumbersome.

Slowly but surely, his horns retracted – all those small, bony appendages that gave his features unique definition. Mack let his maw hang open, running his tongue around his mouth and the insides of his teeth, though he tried to be careful of the sharp points. However, there were fewer and fewer sharp edges as his jaw throbbed painfully, his teeth retracting, pulling back into his jawbone.

"Nngghhh..."

He'd never made a groan like that before and Mack almost chuffed a laugh at himself. He would have done so too if his tongue didn't feel as strange in his mouth as it did in that moment, his tail losing mobility, sweep by slow sweep.

The dragon pushed back up and away from the ledge, moving slowly and carefully, thinking about where he put each foot and balanced on his hands, steadying his body. He didn't want to slip, oh no, not as he eased himself back, a strange warmth flowing through him. That was not something that he had expected, as if liquid honey was warming his veins, his toes flexing and curling as he dug his claws into the rough stone. Although he could not cut into the stone of the mountaintop, the edge where he was poised, he left deep scratches in it.

There would be no other evidence of his transformation as he stood there, eyeing his hands as his jaw reshaped itself. His head grew smoother and rounder, his horns drawing all the way back into his skull, everything lighter. Mack had never considered just what it would feel like to not have his horns, even if he had been the one who had chosen the potion, trying to smile even as his lips turned hard and unyielding.

"Unngghh… I didnuh… Mmmph? Hehah…"

Oh, he had to laugh at himself, amusement bubbling up in the back of his throat. He held out his arms before him, turning his head a little more to the side so that he could better take them in with one eye, his eyes shifting, ever so slightly, towards the sides of his head. They would still have a minorly forward-facing turn, of course, the eyes of a predator species, but avians, after all, typically had a more wide-ranging field of view than dragons.

Often, but not always. He would soon find out just how he was to transform…

The prickling tingle and tickle of his scales was swiftly revealed to be the features coming into place, though each scale transformed into a feather individually. The drake squirmed and shuddered, shifting his weight from foot to foot, his claws digging down, but even his feet were becoming slenderer, finer, the feet of a bird. He'd still have claws there, though it was fascinating, even as he tried to take in every transformation at once, but they would be different.

A red kite, after all, had more spindly legs, so his slimmed down, yellow "scales" formed on the lower half of his legs, not needing to cover all that much. His first toe merged with the second, sucking together as if they had been glued, and Mack chittered faintly, wriggling them just to see how they felt. His heel pushed out, slim and birdlike, tipped with a talon as his own talons grew a little less curved, dark and slender.

The feather transformation felt like the most far sweeping over his body, even though growing a beak was enticing too, all in how his jaw rounded, losing the bone in lieu of the beak. He gasped for a moment when his nostrils shifted to the 'nares of a bird's beak, his respiratory system needing to rearrange a little, but the first breath of fresh, clean air through them helped a lot.

"Mmm…"

His tongue felt like it was a little pointed, transforming slowly, not a tongue that was meant to push things down his throat anymore. It ran around the inside of his beak, marvelling at the smoothness there, how hard the beak felt, when he had thought teeth were the most fearsome of all. The tip of his beak hooked viciously, sharp enough to tear into meat and crush bone, for a red kite, before the evolution of them as anthros, was a scavenger bird, making the most of any felled prey that it found.

The feathers, however… They were what he longed for. His arms fell stiff, pressed out a little from his body, as his shoulders and shoulder blades thickened with muscle, pushing his traps back out by tensing them. Yet they stayed there, the muscle reinforced, a deep ache rising from his back as new bone formed, layering down his arms to better support where they were to turn into multi-functioning wings and arms. It may not have been heavy bone, not as the bone in the rest of his body too hollowed out and lightened, but it was still there: delicate and yet perfectly suited to the purpose that it was formed for.

Every scale drew into a perfect feather, a rich brown and darker on top around his shoulders and down his back, fading to mottled cream and brown around his belly and sides. He hastened, too late, to get his shirt off as his growing wings tickled his shirt, which had some room into which to grow, though it was the ones under the armpits that prickled out a little too much. Mack's shirt tugged as he struggled to get it around his transforming arms, belatedly wishing that he had started nude. At least he was not transforming into a non-anthropomorphic form, as that would have most likely ripped his clothes, unless he shrank down.

That heat was still there, however, even as his tail tickled and he tried to glance back, spreading his transforming wing-arms for balance. There didn't seem to be much balance at all for the transforming dragon-bird to take, however, as he ran his tongue temptingly against the edge of his beak, his tail lighter and lighter, losing the bone, even though it did not shrink. Where the feathers filled in the gaps on his body, between the ones where his scales had transformed first, it ached with the quill drawing out from his body, though he was lucky that he was not transforming with a protective sheath over each feather. That would have been exceedingly uncomfortable, though Mack was not to know.

"Mmm…"

It was easier to talk with a beak, though he had to use his tongue more to control how his words sounded. That was not what the transforming anthro had in mind, however, for he was not interested in talking, spreading his wing-arms as the long, primary, flight feathers tickled down. They filled out his new wings as his heart surged. They may have not been the back-wings that his father had, but they were more than enough, feathered and, temporarily, all his own.

His head swung, light and easy, and he flapped his wing-arms, stretching and straining, feeling out the peculiar sensation of the feathers tickling into place. Somehow, he even got a drop of sensation as they fanned out, his tail flattening into a long, feathered tail instead of a thick, muscular one. It was not brown-feathered, however, darker on top with a lighter underside – and if he could have seen his face, he would have seen where it was a greyer manner of brown, the feathers melding seamlessly with the richer shades around his neck and upper back.

"Mmm…"

It was still hard to talk and there was something tugging his attention downward, something sucking back into his body. Mack's eyes widened and the, mostly bird, shoved his trousers down, half struggling out of them, though he already could see enough.

He had had a small sheath before, though it drew smoothly back into his body, the slit remaining as his balls retracted too. They would be tucked up into his lower abdomen, safely protected and aerodynamic, and Mack wouldn't have to worry about them in the slightest.

"Oh… What?"

Mack swung his head back and forth as his transformation settled over him: an anthro red kite, a bird of prey, with a wicked beak and a gleam in his eye. The muscles across his back were strong enough to pump and power his wing-arms, although he was yet to try them out, his feathers so fresh and clean and new as he stepped out of his trousers. At least his shoes were sitting beside him already, so he had not had to worry about his claws cutting into those as he transformed.

They were so different too, skinny and flexible, curling around as if he could grip branches with his feet, though Mack was not interested in working that out, no. He didn't care about things like that, not as he flapped his wing-arms, delighting in the gust of air that poured around him.

He sucked in a breath, heart lifting – yet that did not take his attention away from the tension at the slit where his cock was. It was lower down than he had expected and he would later learn that, in that body, he had a modified cloaca, though it allowed a cock to be tucked away inside too. Every transformation potion, like the huge variety of anthro bodies, was different and there was a wealth for the dragon to explore and enjoy.

Who knew? One day, he might even keep his wings…

The slender length of his cock pressed out – but it wasn't his cock either, at the same time. It was pinker and smoother, tapered to a narrow point – and it didn't have any of the draconic ridges along it. Mack clicked the edges of his beak together temptingly, hardly noticing it while his attention was drawn downward and he blushed under the feathers of his cheek.

"Mmmph…"

Arousal was not something = he had expected from a transformation like that, though he relished in it, letting everything come as it wanted. Flying would come soon enough, flapping and pumping his wings slowly, testing out just how they moved, how he could scoop and shape the air with them. It was better to try out things like that, after all, on the ground, even while his hand slowly curled around his cock.

"Oh…"

Mack trembled. His hands too… They still had claws, tiny talons with a slight curve to them, but they were feathered too. The feathers there were so small and so delicate that he could not resist the urge to brush them up in the wrong direction, just to explore the softer, downy underlayer.

The top ones had to have some kind of waterproofing, a gleaming sheen to them. But Mack wasn't thinking about that as his tail feathers fanned out excitedly, curling his talons and scraping up the rock a little more.

The breeze caught him as he brought himself higher and higher, stroking his hand up and down his shaft, the smoothness catching him. Oh, but he was so sensitive! He had barely even thought that a different member could bring with it so many different sensation, even the pulse of blood within his shaft achingly delicious.

He moaned and let his head fall back, wild out there, no one to bear witness to him. Mack would not have even stopped if he had been come upon by hikers, his tail flicking lightly as if he was still trying to use it like a dragon's tail, but he had to get used to the lesser weight of it.

Maybe. In time. His hand sliding up and down his length was too inviting, his feathers catching, though the newly transformed red kite did not even care when he accidentally tugged one out. It may have brought with it a prick of pain, but it was easy to move by as he huffed and grunted, not able to feel the breath passing over his beak as he exhaled sharply through his 'nares.

"Mmmph… Oh… Yessss…"

He hissed a little, slurring his words, though all would come in time. To have wings… All he had wanted! It was pure, raw delight that surged through him, begging him to pay attention to it, though he had to feed it, yes, to let the urge swell more and more and more.

Mack's long, low groan rolled from him, a trickle of pre-cum dribbling out against his feathered hand. It was truly amazing how anthros had evolved, though he didn't think that the short claws at his fingertips were something that should have remained. He only took care to keep them away from his cock, not wanting to harm himself in the slightest, need rocking desperately through him.

"Mmmm… Oh!"

And then, all in a rush: orgasm. It burst upon him like sunshine upon the mountainside, though the drizzle still beaded on his feathers, misting over him. The red kite let his head fall back, his beak open in a sharp, keening cry, echoing down the mountainside, though it would fade into oblivion before it reached any wandering ears. His tail flicked, the feathers spreading out lustfully, his cock twitching and pulsing, his balls aching inside. He could *feel* where they were held, a coil of tightness locked into his lower abdomen, and pressed his free hand down on it, revelling in the heated throb of fresh sensation.

It rolled through him, spilling spurt after spurt over the ground, tipping forward so he didn't make a mess of his fresh feathers. He grunted thickly, closing his beak, eyes narrowing, blinking away tears that he had not expected to be there. It was just the force of his transformation, however, and the wind pulling at his feathers, striving to strip the moisture from his orbs, but he laughed and wiped it away anyway with the hand not gripping his cock.

Refreshed and whole, he licked his beak and stood tall, relaxing as his shaft retracted into his slit again, the cloaca hiding everything neatly and efficiently. It was time, though Mack had never envisioned needing to have an orgasm before taking his first flight, finally spreading his wings with his heart well and truly in his beak.

It was stupid.

It was reckless.

He was going to do it anyway. Because he believed in himself.

Stepping to the edge of the rock again, he looked down without fear, the world dropping away from him to a lake far, far below. The face of the cliff was not sheer, though it may as well have been, the red kite pumping his wings a couple of times for confidence, testing his balance, just how hard he would have to flap them.

In the end, it did not matter at all as he hurled his light body into a freefall, cascading down with a feral shriek, eyes wide and perfectly focused, seeing further than he ever had before. He spread his wing-arms and caught the wind, soaring, not expending energy, just letting the massive, long feathers carry him up and away, across the mountains themselves. His transformation would last over six hours and he'd return in time to his starting point, knowing where he'd come from without actively considering it in his mind. Just another handy feature of drawing on the instincts of a new species.

Finally taking flight, there would never be any going back for Mack. Not as he tried out transformation after transformation, all until he found the exact right one that suited him.

And that one would be permanent.

# From One Body to Another

Samir stood waist-deep in the lake, the chill of the mountain air sinking into his bones. As a wolf, he was used to being out in the wilds and, honestly, had worked as a park ranger for some time overseas, back when he'd been taking a gap year. The work, back then, hadn't paid all that well for the wolf anthro, but, well, he'd still tried his best to take things forward, to learn all that he could.

What he had learned, over in the States before retreating back to his home country of England, was a little trick. Something like meditation, something like relaxation…but all about changing one form for another.

And, out there, was the perfect spot to do it. With Autumn rolling in, the leaves changing colour, Samir was right where he needed to be, a gentle yet cooling breeze licking at his fur. Only wearing a pair of shorts was perhaps not Samir's wisest idea but, well…the wolf wasn't going to be in that body for long.

"Okay…" He said, though he didn't really need to control himself at all to reach for the unlocked power, what had been so graciously imparted to him a long time ago. "Now… Breathe…in…and out…"

*Relax everything. Let your mind be still. The power is there.*

*You only have to reach for it.*

He knew that, though that didn't make it any easier to claim for his own, breathing as slowly and as steadily as he could, though his sheath was already plumping up within his shorts. Oh, Samir's need was there, it most certainly was, though there were so many aspects to transformation for him to think about.

Would his tail change? Would he retain a wolf-like appearance? Would his first real transformation, of his kin of shapeshifters, take him to such a size that he wouldn't be able to fit in normal homes and buildings?

Samir gulped, his ears splaying, though the wolf managed to stop himself from pinning them flat to his skull. It wasn't what he wanted to do and neither was it what he needed in that moment.

Calm was what he needed. For the transformation was coming whether he felt wholly ready for it or not, even if Samir was well aware that his kind, wolves, had not shifted forms for centuries. That was why he had gone in search of the ability to do so, wanting to bring back just a little of what they had lost.

It was a hope and perhaps a folly, but it would be Samir's own to hold, one way or another. It was all the wolf could try for, as the Autumnal breeze licking at his fur wasn't going to wait. Water lapped around him, moving with a rhythm of its own, only stirred up by the wind. Samir wondered if there was a point that a creek or a river fed into it, though he had not explored that area enough to tell, one way or another.

It was okay though. If all went well, he would soon have a form that would be more than enough to hold him steady in the water.

Perhaps that was a little misplaced confidence, considering the wolf didn't know quite what transformation he was reaching for, only unlocking his power, but he had to believe it was so. The water would help him, supposedly, as it was less grounding in its movements than the earth.

He understood that, letting his mind wander, his dark lips ever so slightly parted as coolness drifted into his mouth, over his tongue and around his sharp teeth. The flow of it was soothing and, in a way, it made him think of other bodies of water that he was more familiar with – like the Towy river where he had fished when he'd been young, on holiday with his family, and the Gower sands, where the beach stretched on and on and on. There were other holidays he'd taken in the west of the country, Wales, but the place names were a little trickier for him to pronounce, not living there all the time. Still, he remembered the touch of water on his fur, lifting it from his body, most of all, a part of him aching to lean into it, to revel in the tease of it flowing between his toes, enticing him to stretch them out into the sand.

There was no sand on the bottom of the lake – at least not where Samir was standing, but he still wriggled his toes, feeling mud and weed sift around them. It was not a pleasant sensation and, still, the wolf remained there, steady in his resolution to find what his kind had lost.

And then it came. It was so subtle that Samir could have missed it, at least at first, his tail stiffening, losing the pull from the base of it that gave his tail its wag. He was not as expressive as a canine anthro with his tail, of course, using it more to signal tension or unsureness in his daily life, but it was still noticeable.

Samir's fingers twitched but all he could do was concentrate on his breathing, inhaling and exhaling very slowly and deeply, his chest rising and falling evenly. Yet with every intake of air, his chest rose just a little bit more, expanding.

"Oh…"

He breathed out, licking the side of his muzzle, his body alive with electric tingles. His claws ached terribly and he rolled his shoulders back, trying to contain himself. Yet Samir was soon to find out that his body was simply not something that could be contained.

It was never supposed to be contained, no, not in the slightest, not as a new form pulled from him. He'd researched his wolf-anthro people as much as he could, though records showed they could transform into a myriad of other creatures. It went back to the

Celts, how they had influenced the culture of what had, in the end, become the United Kingdom – but that was a long story.

He'd see, however, that he had closer ties to Wales than even Samir could have expected. And perhaps all those times spent around the waters of Wales had had more of an influence on him still…

"Yes…"

He breathed slowly and evenly, relaxing in the moment, need rising, even his sheath feeling different. Even though Samir was wearing long shorts, which felt as if they were more than enough to cover him, a sense of exposure curled deep inside, as if he had been stripped down to the very core of his being.

It happened slowly, allowing him to draw on the little details. At first, he thought the wind had picked up, ruffling his grey fur, but, well, it was clearly so much more than that. As the fur flattened against his hide, tucking into scale-like shapes, though every scale pointed down his body, with a tapered edge on the side closest to his tail. Samir sucked in a breath, even though his chest was tight – and larger at the same time.

That didn't make sense, but it didn't have to make sense as the wolf used what he'd learned to call on powers buried deep inside him, letting them swell and pull through him, inflating his chest out and out and out. His scaled body twisted and Samir grunted, trying to look down at himself, even as his neck stiffened.

There was too much going on in his changes, as slow as they were, to absorb everything at once, his jaws hanging open as he moaned.

"Oof…"

It was hard, harder than Samir could ever have thought possible, for he had to keep a hold on his powers and feel everything happening to him. Without a steady reflection to show him what was happening to his body, the transformation came to him through intimate sensation primarily.

His ears twitched, flattening and softening, the sensation of them sucking back into his scalp unnerving. Yet Samir could still hear as tiny indents in the side of his head denoted where his ears were, covered by a thin layer of skin where the scales were smaller and more delicate, tucking into his ear canal. He grunted and resisted the urge to itch at the side of his head as the tiny tunnel of his ear canal burrowed into its rightful place, a little higher on his head than he was used to, but that was okay.

The wolf's skull cracked and groaned as it pressed out, the brow softening and elongating into a shape that surprised him. He'd thought he would remain somewhat wolf-like but, well…maybe that was too much to ask for. All Samir had wanted to do was to find out what was buried inside him, though it was set to surprise him.

It would have been boring if not.

He groaned, tipping forward, holding the left side of his head even as something bulged from the back of his skull, the creak of his bones straining and growing echoing through his head. His forehead pounded with a splitting headache – and then it was gone, his body, somehow, knowing exactly what it needed to do to adjust to the transformation. Bodies could do a lot more than many anthros gave them credit for and, well, his transformation was a prime example of that, it had to be said.

"Unff…"

He huffed, trying to shake his head, but it was too difficult, panic fluttering in the cage of his ribs as his neck stretched out and out and out. Yet it was the crack and pop of his body adding extra vertebrae to his neck and spinal column that stressed him the most, the strain of his body being forcibly pulled into a form he was unfamiliar with merely a byproduct there.

"Nnngghhh… Unff… It's…"

He tried to talk but his tongue twisted, curling around his mouth. And not just in the wolf-like way, no, it twisted back and forth, overly flexible, flicking out as it grew, the tip forked and lashing the side of his muzzle. His head ached fiercely and he reached back blindly, groping, to feel the bony protrusions on the back of his head, how they pointed straight back with sharper points. There was something else under them too, a second set of bony protrusions, but they seemed smaller, a couple more lighter ones still following around the curve of his cheek to the base of his jaw.

*Oh…*

Horns. They were *horns*. That, at least, made sense to him and he tipped his head experimentally back and forth, testing out the weight of them. It was a lot harder to balance with the extra weight added already to one of the heaviest parts of his body (the head was a very important part of balance, surprisingly so) but he supposed he would get used to it. Even if the wolf didn't know for how long he would stay in his new form for – or even if he would be able to change back when he was ready to.

Not having fur was strange, though Samir was not cold. He was aware, however, of the water swilling between his legs, lapping at his thighs, comfortable there, though better able to absorb the changes in temperature around him. Taking a deep, steadying breath, he grunted as his muzzle narrowed and elongated a little further, becoming elegant and refined. His nostrils curved up a little, ridged above them, though there was no moist wetness there anymore, a different way of filtering through scents offered to the wolf.

Yet could Samir even say he was a wolf anymore? It was hard to say when he was poised between two worlds, a foot in one and the other foot firmly planted in the world of being a shapeshifter. He had to take the leap, one way or the other, to find out who he truly was, deep down.

His tongue wormed its way around his mouth, as if it had a mind of its own. It ran around his teeth as they sharpened a little more, though he did not lose the dominance of canines in his mouth, even if they became a little more fang-like. Every tooth remained tucked within his lips, however, for which Samir was thankful. It was just one little thing that he was more comfortable with, even as his jaw narrowed a little more, inhaling sharply through the neat tuck of his new nostrils.

"Hmph…"

Words wouldn't come with a tongue like that and Samir would have to re-learn how to talk with a new muzzle, but that was okay. There was no rush and there was no one there with him either, not even as heat pooled in his lower stomach. He grunted, shifting his weight from hip to hip as the water lapped at him, his tail stiffening and straightening, though only for the transformation.

It flowed down, new muscle bulging to life along it, though it had a smooth, elegant appearance. Only then did Samir come to understand how it was becoming reptilian, though the shades of blue and green laced through his scales did not remind him of any reptile in the world that he already knew of.

He didn't have to be of the known world, after all, not when he was there, well and truly, to step into the unknown, grunting as his neck stretched, filling out like a tube. It reminded him of the change in his tail, though perhaps he needed a longer, thicker tail like that to help balance his neck, even if he did not quite understand.

Samir wobbled, his arms stretching out and out and out, layers of new skin, leathery like hide, stringing from them. It ached as it pulled from him, from his wrist all the way down to his armpit, and he wriggled back and forth, his legs bulking up and filling out with lean, tight muscle.

Yet his whole body was larger, the water stirring around him as he was forced to grow, tipping forward as his weight unbalanced him and splashing down into the water. Somehow, it felt natural to balance on his elbows and hands, gasping, his nose just rising above the surface of the water – yet that was different too. If he had been still a wolf, just a wolf, he would have been dunked under just for toppling forward. But he had got to the size of a horse and still grew, his body filling out and fleshing up, waist tucking sharply up and in.

*What…am I?*

Samir's head swam, though a sense of soft peace washed through him. Maybe it was the movement of the lake around him: so calm and yet so unpredictable at the same time. He could not judge where the water was to be stirred up next, what ripples would come his way, but he was comfortable where he was, letting it all flow around him.

He pulled his head back and up as his neck and tail relaxed, finally able to see himself.

And what greeted him was the face of a great lizard, with a long, refined muzzle, like one that could have possible been used for catching fish. His nostrils were smoothly curved and his eyes itched, even then, as the eyeballs shifted a little further forward, seeking a more predatory gaze. The horns on top of his head no longer felt like they were unbalancing him and a long fin spiked from his neck, leathery and wet, running down his spine from the back of his head, itching his tail as it sprung into place there too.

A dragon. So, the creature inside him, what his kind could shapeshift into…was a dragon. Who would have thought that?

Knowing what he was becoming soothed Samir a little, flutters of excitement bustling around his heart, though he didn't have to worry himself at all. The changes came more smoothly, his power running of its own accord, and he no longer had to concentrate on keeping it right there at the forefront of his mind anymore. He parted his mouth, testing out the stronger muscles there, how the bite power had changed, coolness brushing his cheeks.

Yet the transforming dragon was still going as heat warmed between his legs, his shorts shifting, pulling at his body. He hadn't thought about that, but they dug into his scales, the elastic straining until he twisted around with a low grunt and clawed at them. His hand curved, claws elongating and curling, twisting into longer, grabbing claws – though not too big, for it was the leathery flaps of wings that had stretched down his arms.

*Huh… I thought dragons had wings on their backs…not their arms?*

But Samir was not just any dragon, not as the dragon grunted and huffed, his sheath flattening back against his belly and leaving a slit there. It was as if it was not any matter at all, for his genitals to be smoothly sucked back up inside his body, but he revealed them as those claws, finally, caught at his shorts and tore them away.

He didn't have an anthro definition to his buttocks anymore anyway, the round of them filling out with muscle, the kind of creature that would sit back on their haunches to survey their surroundings. They rounded out with thick muscle, his tail swinging back and forth under the water, stirring it up further as he harried mud from the lake floor, eyeing up the darkening waters. It churned and swirled but would always settle again, if only he was still.

It was the water that helped him change, reminding him of the flow and ebb of the world around him, what he had lost touch with, even though he was a wolf. Yet he was not grounded – and was not supposed to be, not as Samir tested out his new body and spread his wings wide. The leather filled in with spines to support it, allowing him to more easily walk hunched forward, he guessed, as if on his elbows. He'd seen dragons like that before, in books. They'd been called wyverns. Of course, Samir had not thought they'd really existed and had always expected them to be more fearsome, yet the dragon only saw beauty reflected in the rippling, waving water.

Later, he would find a stiller body of water to take in his reflection, huffing and heaving, straining to fill his aching lungs. Yet there was something there, at his loins, that the wyvern could not have expected, his length pressing out of the slit in a slow, tickling slide.

He shuddered. Oh, that was a very different sensation indeed, the pressure of his slit on either side of his draconic cock teasing him even as he grew. His tail thrashed and Samir strove to calm himself, filling his lungs with deep, steadying breaths. Yet nothing was to steady him, not in that moment, not as he grunted and licked his lips, his cock underwater.

His transformation rippled through him as his spine crackled and crunched, his forearms lengthening as more height and bulk was added to his body, everything growing in proportion. Even though he had been standing moderately comfortably in the water before, the dragon swiftly rose from it high enough so that his belly was exposed – and a long, fat length of dragon meat.

It was almost an elegant cock, Samir thought, grunting as it throbbed and slapped against his own stomach, clenching muscles in his lower abdomen that, honestly, he'd never thought about before. It was longer and gave the impression that it was thinner, but it too had grown in proportion to his size, leaving nothing at all to the imagination.

It drooled thickly, more than it ever had done when he'd been a wolf, though Samir had never paid intimate attention to his member before, not like that. He huffed and grunted, licking his lips again, though the sensation of his tongue swiping over the softer lips and then his firmer scales was strange to him. The wyvern would get used to it, water splashing up against him as the wind picked up, stirring up the surface of the lake.

He just had to lean into it, to follow a little more of what instinct was telling him, all while the final details and nuances of his transformation slid into place.

A third eyelid, to protect his eyes when he was flying.

A delicate spike every few inches down his spinal fin, allowing him to control it slightly, adding to his edge of control in the air.

The three spines prickling to life at the very tip of his tail, a weapon that would never be used.

How the edges of every scale seemed to settle just a little more into place, seating themselves firmly into his body.

The wyvern groaned, pumping his muscles, his abdomen flexing and contracting as he rocked his hind end. It was not purely the motion of his hindquarters that made his cock jump and slap against his stomach, though the wyvern had never imagined turning into a creature, technically without any hands or paws that he could use with greater dexterity. With his intelligence in that form, he had to get a little more creative, even if all Samir was doing was following instinct too.

He had to, his need too great, swirling and pooling inside him, clawing at his stomach. It rose stringently, demanding attention, and the wyvern let out a warbling little whimper as it swelled higher and higher, greater and greater. His cock dripped and drooled, splattering pre-cum with every slap of his shaft up against his own abdomen, needing it increasingly, every passing second serving to heighten his desire.

"Unff…"

Grunts and groans rose a little more easily from his lips as Samir got to grips with his voice box, huffing and moaning, words whispering forth. His cock jerked against his belly, the tip splattering pre-cum in pearly beads, though every drop swiftly dissipated the moment it hit the water as an individual. Need flared inside, swirling in the pit of his stomach, and he kept going, following the whims of a body that he was still very much yet to understand.

Such as it was, orgasm caught the dragon off-guard. One moment he was jerking and slapping his cock up against his own stomach and the next he was snarling and snapping at empty air, losing control, his cock jetting off with long, thick loads of cum, painting the water. His seed swirled into it, holding its form and shape for a fraction of a moment before dissipating, his tail winding back and forth rapidly, though it hung down to balance him there, standing in the water.

The wyvern panted heavily, relishing in climax, in every throb that drummed through him, pulse after pulse. His testes were held internally that time, though he still felt as if something was contracting back there, maybe the muscles right at the tops of his inner thighs pulsating a little, pulling in with every grind and thrust.

Samir did not care for how much he churned up the water or that he was out in the open, confident that no one would see him. There was a risk, however, minute, but the shapeshifter languished in his transformation, adoring it, huffing and panting as he came back down.

Slowly but surely, licking his lips, eyelids fluttering, Samir came back to himself. Yet a glow of pleasure swept through him, as if his whole body was immersed in warm water, swilling around him, swelling lusciously. He could linger there for as long as he liked, his tail steadying him, jaws parted in a gentle, wyvern-like smile.

In uncovering the legacy of his kind, Samir stepped into a new way of being. The transformed wolf-dragon, however, had never considered just how much pleasure there was to be had in transforming.

That changed everything…

The wyvern smiled.

And there was so much yet for him to discover.

# From Man to Phoenix

Since transformation potions had come out on the market, Remy hadn't honestly found anything that appealed to him. Sure, he had read all those kids transformation books when he'd been younger and some of those horror-themed ones too and been fascinated by them – but he'd never really thought that they would apply to him.

When it came to kinks as an adult, that was.

He took his time in the sex shop, confident in the knowledge that he was as good as anonymous there: no one truly cared what anyone who was shopping there did, he knew. Remy, at least, was glad he had worked that out when he was a little younger, because it wasn't at all something that he wanted to be worrying about at all.

Hey, he was just there looking for something, after all, to have a little solo fun with.

Ah!

Remy paused, a smirk breaking across his face, though it dipped and swayed as if it was shy to be seen there. A transformation potion… And a new one at that! It was not of the usual things (no one had been surprised what kinks had come out first and foremost on that side of things, truly) but just what he wanted.

Not furry, not monstrous, not overtly sexual… Just beautiful. A form that he could well and truly lean into and, of course, enjoy.

With a smile, Remy trotted up to the cashier with just the single potion clasped in his hand.

"Just this, please."

His evening was going to be a lot more entertaining than he'd before expected.

And Remy didn't waste any time at all getting things started, darting up the steps to his flat on getting home and dumping his bag just inside the door.

*Oh, I've been waiting for this…*

Sure, he had been trying out the usual transformations, furry stuff mostly and a bit of the monsters when he was just getting into actual transformation, but there would be nothing like trying out a spot of glory too. Something beautiful, something seductive…keeping both his sex and gender, of course. That side wasn't quite what Remy was into.

He took the potion, though, for him, it was only a mouthful. He upended the bottle, clasping the lip between his teeth, trying to prod and poke with his tongue into the smooth, glass interior.

He had to get every last little drop out, after all. It wouldn't be worth it, not for him, if even a single feather was out of place.

"Mm… What now then?"

Fidgeting in the kitchen, he shook his head, not knowing what else to do. A lot of the other transformation potions and pills that he had tried out before had been fast acting and the problem with them had been just how long they lasted. Some had barely even allowed him ten minutes of transformation fun before reverting to his usual, boring form.

And Remy just wanted plenty of time for himself, leaning on the kitchen counter as he eyed up the couple of dishes in the sink. Maybe there was time to do them before he transformed?

A tingle ran through him, making him spread the fingers of his left hand out flat on the surface.

"Ohhh…"

He hissed through his teeth, shifting his weight from foot to foot, feeling like something was moving behind him, swaying lightly from side to side. It was strange, a weight there that had no place on his body, yet he could not prevent the prickle of excitement rising from his stomach, spreading and shuddering through his entire body. In a way, it was as if he had injected the transformation potion, feeling it spread out through his body through the network of his veins.

In reality, from the research he had done, it was more intricate than that. Yet Remy wasn't about to let his mind wander to any of that as his need rose, licking his lips, his head swirling and spinning pleasantly with tender need.

"Oh… Yes… This… *This* is what I wanted…"

He languished there, slowly removing his T-shirt, though Remy loathed dragging it up over his head. It felt like it was catching on something even then, pulling too close to his body, and he hissed through his teeth.

For, as he tried to strip down and didn't quite get there, tiny feathers grew all over his body. It was not entirely comfortable as the new quills sprouted, though Remy could only be glad that the feathers were not wrapped in the sheaths that new feathers would usually be clad in – if he was really a bird growing a replacement feather, that was. From one of his earlier experiences with avian transformation, that had proven to be a most painful experience.

Realistic though. He had to give the creators of the transformation potion, back then, credit for that.

"Mmm…"

Remy groaned, arching his back as his spine stretched – just a little. It was not growing into a tail that he would be able to curl back and forth like a cat or even a snake, but one that would be needed to control the tail feathers set to sprout there. He shivered. How long would they be? Would they be big enough for him to fan up over his back, surrounding himself in shimmering delight – kind of like a peacock?

Ah, but he would be more glorious than that, smiling even as his face grew a little stiffer, his lips firmer, as if the flexibility was going to be gone from them soon. There had to be concessions in transformation, after all, trading one form for another, and he relaxed into it.

His lips and his face… Remy grunted softly in the back of his throat as his lips hardened up, his face shrinking in around it. Not much – but enough that it felt like he was being squeezed, even the man's skull crinkling and crackling lightly as it grew smaller.

"Mmph…"

He shuddered, resisting the urge to curl forward, his shoulders hunching, a rippling tremor running through him. Something pressed in around his neck, squeezing and allowing it to lengthen a little more, though it was all part of the show.

"Nngghhh…"

He grunted, shaking his head, lips opening and closing as they transformed into a beak, stretching up into the corner of his jaw, though it was a different framework than what he was used to. The crunch at the corner of his jaw had him flinching and he gulped hard, though his tongue was still there, slimming down softly to fill the base of his beak, the tip of it narrowed to a round, smooth point, though it was not hooked or sharp like that of a bird of prey.

It did not need to be. For the creature that he was transforming into was a phoenix and they fed off sustenance beyond anything that a mortal could ever have locked onto.

Gasping, he struggled to get out of his jeans, his fingers heavily feathered, though they would not be as useful as the hands he knew for very much longer. His arms grew heavier and heavier, shimmering purple and blue feathers layering every surface as they spread up his neck and over his head too.

*Huh… I kind of thought they'd be…golden?*

But Remy was more than happy with how his transformation was turning out, a long tail sprouting into his jeans. He chirped and clacked the edges of his beak together uncomfortably as he rolled his weight from one foot to the other, losing control – yet control was not his to be taken in a moment like that, after all. That was why people had to be careful to only buy from reputable traders. Though some black-market ones could be entertaining from time to time too, if one was feeling like a little bit of a risk...

Not that time, however. Remy just wanted to relish in it, even as his tail squashed into his jeans, the heavy material cloying and hampering its growth as he clicked his beak in frustration. It was just hard to get them off in time when his eyes were shifting, slowly, a little more to the sides of his head, his vision blurring, eyes watering around the edges. There was still a tear duct there, but it grew larger, tiny, delicate feathers framing the orbs.

Oh, he wished he was able to see just how he was transforming, yet it was better that way. When he could not see, he had to luxuriate in sensation, how the muscles across his chest gently bulked up – though not to the point that anyone would have considered it out of place on an avian. It was just a broader chest, his pectoral muscles more defined with a line between and around them, than what he was used to, his shoulders rounding out lightly.

He could not fly as a phoenix, unfortunately, but the long feathers running down his arms made him feel like he could, as if it would be oh so very easy just to spread his arms wide and let those long, primary feathers swell softly into place. The flight feathers came in too, prickling less stringently now that he had the base feathering of his new body in place, but the pulling sensation of each one stretching and growing into place sent little ripples through him.

"Mmm…"

Even Remy's voice was different, a little higher pitched before. He shoved his jeans down enough so that they pooled around each foot, though even those were changing when he had not managed to get his shoes off in time.

Remy should really have thought about that, though there was still time to roughly and crudely kick them off, even as his toes slimmed down. His underwear had mostly come down with his jeans, allowing him to brush a shaking hand over his crotch, teasing his shaft with the back of his hand. It was only brief, however, as his shaft shrank, pulling back more and more into his feathered crotch, bristling in a teasing swathe of violet and turquoise, the feathers shimmering as he turned. Every one seemed to catch the light a little differently and Remy would have been more than glad to spend hour after hour examining every little feather on his body, teasing and preening every single one.

It was all part of the transformation, the in-depth body exploration, testing out how his centre of balance changed and even those smaller, more subtle changes in musculature affected how he moved. No one that didn't have such a liking for transformation would have appreciated that.

And that was fine… He was there to enjoy it, his shaft smoothing down as if it had never been. But his body shifted inside, forming a cloaca that was well-framed by protective feathers between his legs. It contained everything in one hole – though was not quite what he was used to, even as Remy chuckled breathlessly and turned around, his back to the kitchen counter, the top of his buttocks just about reaching it.

*Funny, I feel a little smaller…*

But he'd check out his height later, if that was even something he was interested in. His cloaca was soft, so sensitive between his legs, and Remy could not resist feeding a finger into it, pressing deeper and gently swirling it around as he tested out the new feature of his body.

"Oh… Ohhhh!"

It was good, too good – perhaps even more so than it had any right to be. He keened out softly, surprised even by the shrill cry that broke his beak – though Remy didn't want to stop, oh no. No… He wanted more, his tail growing, longer and longer, the feathers right at the tip a little curly, as if they were going to spread out, flickering back and forth when he was in movement. Just how much time of his transformation would Remy end up spending strutting back and forth in front of the mirror remained to be seen, fanning his tail out and testing out just how far he could swish it back and forth.

It would prove to be hypnotic, though even the weight of it was such too in that moment, the phoenix clicking his beak, sweeping his tongue lightly around the inside of it. There was not all that much to the transformation, for it was not as if he was growing extra limbs. No… The biggest change, ultimately, was in the feathers, and he smoothed body hands down his chest to his flat stomach, the abdominal muscles contracted there, showing their definition. A bird, after all, had to be designed as light for flight, even though he wasn't intending to see if he could fly (and fall) off any high buildings.

Heat pooled deliciously in his crotch, wet between his legs, moisture seeping softly from his cloaca to mark the feathers at the edge of it. Yet Remy did not spare a moment quite yet as he shivered, his tail stretching out and out and out. Reaching the backs of his knees, it fanned out further, larger across than his torso, and his legs slimmed down, giving him the light, delicate feet and talons of an avian.

His feathers ended at his knees, all below them with the strange, scaley skin of a bird. Yet they were strong, the bones hollow and powerful enough to hold him even when they seemed like they should have been so light and easy to snap. Remy clicked and shivered, his tail growing more and more, his thighs slimming down a little, though there was not a spare ounce of fat left on his body.

It wasn't needed, no, not on a body that should have been designed to fly.

*Maybe I'll have to find a dragon transformation trigger next time…* Remy thought dimly, though it was hard to dredge up thoughts through the overflow of euphoria clawing at him. *Mm… Then I can really…fly…*

That was a challenge for another day, as he rubbed his fingers between his thighs again, seeking out the tease of his cloaca. It was so strange to miss his shaft, but his balls too had been tucked inside – well, kind of like internally held testes.

That was something that he would have to investigate another time, relaxing into the moment as two fingers pressed into his body.

Why did it always feel like Remy was just along for the ride when he indulged in transformation? Oh, but it did not matter really, maybe because transformation was something that could not be called a halt to once it had begun, drawing him along with it so that he was forced to experience every last little detail.

He could do that, just about, letting it sweep him away, licking the edge of his beak cautiously, testing out all the new, subtle nuances of the phoenix's body: his body.

If only for a time.

Yet Remy could not help himself from leaning back against the kitchen counter for support, his body lean and lithe and utterly beautiful in every way he could have imagined. His transformation settled fully over him as his tail feathers stretched out as far as they could, brushing the floor behind his heels, but the final change was the crest atop his head. It flurried out in a tickle of feathers, large and dominant, as if it was there to show off his form to all that cared to see him. It would have made him stand out above a crowd, bobbing along, at least a foot tall, yet so light that Remy barely even felt the weight of it atop his head.

And that was the way that it needed to be. He exhaled softly, his eyes half-closed, letting his beak hang open even though he breathed through the nares on it mostly, which were like nostrils – just for birds.

"Mmm…"

With a new body to take his fancy, he stroked up into his cloaca, finding a sensitive spot and grinding over it. Every new twist of his fingers brought a fresh rush of pleasure, despite Remy not quite knowing what he was doing with a body like that. The last time he'd taken on an avian transformation, he had kept his cock. Having a cloaca was something entirely new.

Yet his skin prickled all over with the fluffing up of his feathers, a need like no other coursing through the phoenix with every beat of his heart. It was not to be held back, no, and the mere act of transformation itself had riled him up to such a point that it did not take all that much stimulation to get him rocking and thrusting, close to the edge in no time at all.

"Unff… Ohhhh…"

He groaned, though it was still of a higher pitch than before, grunting, groaning, letting everything roll through him. All he had to do was be there to experience every last second, from the hitch of breath in his lungs to how the feathers layering his wing-arms ruffled lightly. His fingers were blended into the end of his wing-arms, still there but more difficult to use with the stimulation from the feathers rubbing against each one.

Pressing on, he hunched forward, tail feathers fluttering. Any mere bare semblance of control that he might have thought he still had over himself went well and truly out the window as he moaned and let his head fall back, beak parting, ecstasy breaking within his body. The flood was not to be stopped and he let it come, wave after wave crashing through him as if he was dipping and diving above a raging ocean, his wings spread to capture the spray of saltwater licking at them.

Pulse after pulse of liquid desire swelled within his body, slickening around his fingers as he worked them haplessly back and forth, striving with all his might to push his orgasm on for as long as possible.

Panting heavily, he parted his beak, a gleam in his eyes. For the pleasure was still there, ebbing as he drove his fingers in deeper, a third testing out the limits of his cloaca.

He didn't know how long he'd be able to enjoy the magnificence of a phoenix, after all... So, he'd best enjoy it while he could.

That was the way of it, after all, in feathered brilliance.

# Transforming into a Stud

"Mmm…" Harvey groaned as Vee took down his cock, the wolf's ears softly splayed but not folded back as his tongue caressed the otter's length. "Ohhhh… Are you really sure you want this?"

The wolf grinned up at him, his smooth, grey fur with a darker sheen to it, now that he was shifting to his winter coat in the latter part of the year, darker along the shoulders and back. With a decanter of whisky and a couple of empty glasses on the side table in the living room, they were well on their way to getting all the fun with one another that they wanted that night. Yet even in the most long-term of relationships, a couple had to seek other things to spice things up…

Harvey smiled as Vee came up for air, a string of pre-cum and saliva connecting his lips to the otter's cock, though only for a moment. With their clothes already off, fur bare to the room, they could have carried on as normal.

If not for the transformation pill, contained in its own, tiny bottle, that Vee had brought home for Harvey: a precursor to all the fun that they planned to have together. Harvey was not small at all, when it came to his shaft and balls, though he had always wondered what it would be like to be bigger.

And that was just why Vee wanted to offer him the chance to do more, the wolf smirking as he laid his muzzle on the otter's thigh and gave him the best puppy dog eyes he could muster.

"Mmmm… Yeah, if you want to, honey," he grunted, tongue slipping out to stroke teasingly over the otter's inner thigh. "You don't have to, I just saw it and thought of you, you know – because of what you said before. If you don't want to try it, that's good too. Says it lasts a couple of hours, so not like it will be permanent or too long or anything like that."

Words could have come a little more clearly if they hadn't had those glasses of whisky, though the otter and the wolf were not worried about little things like that. It didn't matter, not in the slightest, as Harvey grunted and leaned back, Vee's nose questing a little higher.

"Okay… I'm ready."

The otter took the initiative, taking the bottle and dropping the pill into the palm of his paw. It only took a moment for him to slip it between his lips, using his tongue to scoop it to the back of his mouth and gulp it down.

It was where it belonged, where it was needed, his breath hitching and catching, eyes wide.

"Oh…"

He really hadn't expected it to work that quickly! It was instant, as if the mere contact of the pill against his oesophagus was enough to kick it all off.

Vee rubbed his thigh soothingly, pressing the tip of his nose into the otter's balls, inhaling deeply.

"It's okay, Harvey," he grunted, licking his lips. "I'm here, relax into it… Oh, you're going to look even more amazing than you already do…"

Harvey barely heard him, relaxing a little more where he was sat, pointing his knees out, allowing the wolf to more easily tuck himself between them. The otter blinked and let his head roll from one shoulder to the other, his body rippling and pulsing softly.

It was as if his flesh did not belong to him anymore, bubbling as it rearranged itself. But that was only because the softer parts of his body had to layer themselves more smoothly over the firm rise of new muscle. Harvey groaned and clenched his paws, curling his toes, trying to relax into it, as Vee had said, though it was difficult when the burn felt like when he was pushing himself swimming. Of course, it was hard to push himself to that point, being an otter and all, though he still recalled the feeling of pain and heat prickling through his muscles.

It was strange, even looking down at his body, the hairs retracting, no longer boasting the waterproof layer. They thinned, better designed to expel heat from the body rather than stop water reaching it and provide an insulating layer, and, fascinated, the otter ran the flat of his paw over his stomach.

"Oh…"

"Mmmm, look at your cock…"

He'd had a small, tucked up sheath before, but all that changed too, though Harvey struggled to focus on everything in his body transforming at once. As his muscles swelled, growing increasingly defined from his shoulders down his triceps to his biceps and forearms, his sheath plumped up and softened – all to contain a much bigger cock. Every pump of blood that was sent into his transforming dick came with a fresh throb of pleasure, as if it was washing through him, yet it smoothed down into a fleshy, pink length. A few speckles of dark grey remained around the base of it, right at the point where it disappeared into the fatter sheath, but that was not his focus.

Not as Harvey's face bulged out, his nostrils widening, bones crunching faintly as his skull was lightly forced into a new shape. He didn't quite know what he was transforming into, though from the pill bottle he knew he was supposed to be big and studly, a more masculine version of himself. That kind of transformation built on who he was as a fur, so there would still be some features of the otter left behind.

Like his eyes, staying the same colour, the same slender feel remaining in his body, even though he bulked up with muscle. It was all to do with the way the transforming otter held himself, for Harvey did not have to hold on to an old form when he could try out a new body for a little while.

His cock, however… Well, it had to draw his focus, even as his fur lightened to a softer shade of brown, smooth and showing off every single muscle in his body from neck to ankle. And there was so much of it on his whole body too, even his pecs seeming to press out a little more, coming apart to show the lines of definition between them, his shoulders broader. The sensation of his bones shifting and growing a little more, though he only ended up gaining a couple of inches in height in the end, was disconcerting, sending crackling, crunching shudders through his frame.

"Unff…"

"Don't worry, Harvey," Vee breathed, nudging his cock with a curiously questing nose. "Mmm… You're amazing, so wonderful… I can't wait to see you fully transformed. You're turning into a bull, Harvey, my bull… Oh my god…"

The wolf clearly could not restrain himself for a single moment more and that was more than okay with the otter – well, could he really call himself that anymore? He was to remain male, of course, but there was something more at play there, something that would allow Harvey to step into a bigger and bolder body than ever before.

He took a deep breath, relaxing into the chair. How could he be so aware of the weight of his body at a time like that? It didn't feel like it should have been possible and yet even the "bull" could feel his buttocks transforming, becoming larger, thicker, the muscle giving them shape that his lean, otter's body simply had not had before. His tail slimmed down slowly, though it had not been all that thick as an otter's rudder, and his breath hitched as he shuddered, not quite able to take a full breath as it tugged languidly at the base of his spine.

"Ohhhh…"

"Mm, that's right, enjoy it… Fuck, this is all so hot…"

He lifted a trembling paw, though did not dare look down at that moment and rocked back against the back of the big, comfortable chair, which was large enough for him to spread out a little on. His fingers twitched and groped for Vee's head, finding the wolf's ears and sliding between them.

Even if Harvey wanted to feel everything, to take in every tiny, treacherously minute detail of his transformation, he could hold Vee too. He could connect with the wolf, even in that moment, his ears twitching to catch the swish of the wolf's grey tail fluff sweeping across the carpet: a light rustle that simply could not be mistaken for anything else. Yet it was the tantalising stroke of Vee's tongue caressing the throbbing length of his cock, again and again, that dragged him into the moment.

He had to be present there, even though there was a strange, distant part of his mind that wanted to disassociate from everything happening, to slip away to another time and place as if he had no physical presence there at all. It was easy for that to happen when one was transforming; fortunately, Harvey had been through enough small transformations for that not to be so much of an issue anymore. He knew how to ground himself, to steady his breath and take long, deep inhales, spending time on the exhale too, feeling every part of his body.

The curl of his fingers, how the tips were growing heavier, almost duller.

The swell of muscle down his thighs, narrowing to a point above his knee.

His lips growing thicker and softer, a new tongue fleshing out within his mouth.

The wolf's lips parting around the rounded, smooth head of his cock.

"Ohhhh… Fuuuck…"

He wasn't able to enunciate as clearly as he would have liked, though that was no problem at all as his tail tried to flick, ropier and tucked under his backside. If it had not been trapped by his glutes, he would have been swinging it back and forth at that very moment, testing out just how the new limits of his body worked.

Yet the bull's attention locked down and on to the wolf's hot muzzle enveloping his cock, even as it transformed. Of course, that was exactly where Vee's attention was going to go and Harvey did not mind that at all, his sloppy, wet tongue flicking out and trying to sweep along the edge of his lips, the outside of his muzzle. He didn't have as much control over his body as he had before, though that was all fine: it would come in a few minutes, surely, of being present in his new body.

"Unnnfff…"

He clenched his jaw, eyelids flickering apart as he looked down at Vee, his vision blurry. His eyes shifted, growing a little larger and rounder, absorbing more light. The eyes of a prey species, after all, had to be big to spot predators coming, even if that was not so much of a problem for anthros those days. Old features from when they had been in the wild, many, many thousands of years ago, remained, however.

That was okay though as he tried to rock his hips up and forward, to spear his growing cock into the wolf's mouth. It was harder than expected and he moaned openly, his jaw hanging slack, allowing his transforming teeth freedom to shift and move. The sharp teeth of an otter, after all, were not needed for a bull and they eased down into molar-like teeth, the teeth of a herbivore.

At least he wouldn't have to eat in his transformed form, for Harvey most definitely didn't want to give up his heavily fish-based diet.

That wasn't what he was transforming for as he spread his fingers out on the back of the wolf's head, his cock swelling within Vee's mouth. He was surprised that the wolf was taking him as deep as he was already, the tip prodding softly into the back of the wolf's throat. Vee, however, was a pro at deep throating big cocks and frequently would show off his skills with big toys before they used them on one another: all hygienic, of course. He wasn't about to worry about anything like that, however, while he was enjoying spending time with his partner.

No… Everything was just the way they wanted it to be, Vee gulping softly around his cock as the head pressed into the back of his throat. They needed it, both of them, and the wolf curling his tongue around as much of the bull's growing dick as he could.

It was tantalising, just how heat rushed to his cock, throbbing on Vee's tongue. It was something they had done many times before, but he had never had his cock sucked and pleased like that while in the middle of a transformation. So, it was something new, just another new experience to add to their list, panting and whimpering, the wolf's tongue fluttering up deliciously against the underside of Harvey's cock.

"Ohhhh…"

Vee languidly bobbed his head on the bull's cock, seeming to savour it. Yet the overload of pleasure was almost too much for Harvey as he grunted thickly in the back of his throat, his balls feeling like they were rounding out more and more. Too much cum churned within them, a throbbing pulse that, honestly, didn't feel like it belonged. Beyond the dull ache of need, wanting to fuck, Harvey didn't usually feel all that much from his nuts – and that was just fine with him. Yet the transformation had to be understood by his mind in some way as he groaned deeply, his tail twitching where it was still partly trapped by his body, need rising more and more.

Too much cum overfilled his nuts, cock throbbing within the wolf's muzzle. Right then and there, he wanted to thrust, to grind in hard and fast, cramming every inch of his still growing dick. Of course, for him, it was just him and Harvey, no one else – and the bull didn't think that he would ever want anyone other than the wolf. It was just the nature of their relationship coming through, the two of them completely committed to one another.

So, he could take it all in, his face moulding into a new form, flesh shifting on the sides of his muzzle, coming down around a soft, damp nose. The bull groaned, his ears pulling out, becoming softer and flappier, not so small and tucked down against his head. As an otter, they had been barely noticeable at all, his entire body lean and dynamic for cutting through the water. His tail thickened slightly at the base, the additional weight and substance there pushing up against his rump, a rougher tuft of hair forming at the tip. It would not be needed for fly swatting in Harvey's case, however…

His toes tried to curl down, yet they hardened up, becoming firm and unyielding, moulding into the shape of cloven hooves, with a gap in the middle, as if they were separated into two hoof-toes. Yet it was just the natural shape of a bull's "foot" and he pressed up as if onto his old toes, the flat form of his foot shifting so that the joint came up higher, giving him a "hock" at the back of his legs.

It would be challenging to walk like that, but, well, his partner didn't seem like he wanted to give Harvey any chance at all to walk while he was transforming. The wolf grunted and groaned around him, drooling messily, yet such messy matters were not any of their concerns, for everything could be cleaned up later, if any problems did indeed come to be. He moaned, nose tipping down, ears twitching back and forth as he found a greater level of control over their movement, yet the bull's eyes were on the wolf.

He couldn't look away, a part of him marvelling at the raw magnitude of his meat grinding in and out of the wolf's mouth. How could he be so big? And he was still as sensitive as ever! His sheath pulled taut around the base of his cock as if it could not strain enough around the base, not quite, yet his body was still comfortable, very much so, as the weight and tenor of transformation settled into the bones and muscles of his body.

Everything was right, just the way it was supposed to be, grunting and groaning, struggling to stand with the last details pulling into place, his tongue flicking out, teasing against his lower lip.

"Unff... Ohhhh..."

"Mmmm?"

Vee almost rolled his eyes back into his head as he looked up at Harvey questioningly, but there was no reason for the bull to stop, not right then. He was there for the moment, for the sensation of his fat length of fuck meat grinding into his lover's muzzle. Oh, and what a muzzle it was, now that he had a cock, however temporary the whole thing was, to really please him, to show him exactly what he was all about, everything that could possibly be done with a magnificent prick like that.

It was his…and not his at the same time. And that was okay too, for they were into transformation to experience more bodies, more things that more bodies could do. Was he repeating himself? Ah, it was no matter. His head was a little fuzzy, pressing his tongue briefly to the roof of his mouth and sweeping it around, feeling out the new edges of his teeth.

Yet the weight of having a new body didn't stop him from staggering, weakly, awkwardly, to his hooves and leaning over the wolf. The wolf's eyes widened, but Vee grabbed at him, fingers digging into his taut, firm buttocks as he encouraged him on. And Harvey more than knew what to do.

Every muscle settled into place, the thicker, chunkier hoof-like tips of his fingers finally feeling useful again, a ropey tail swinging back and forth behind him, as if it needed to move to release some modicum of the tension from his body. Yet he had to thrust, driven by that need, panting through an open mouth – the mouth of a bull.

Harvey would not be an otter again for some time, but that was all well and good. There was not much he needed to worry about there, no, not at all. He grunted and thrust, deep, guttural, masculine sounds leaping from his lips, reverberating in his throat. It was harder than ever to hold back, yet there was not much of the bull that even wanted to. All he wanted was to languish in every last second of the experience, to revel in the slick feel of the wolf's tongue and lips on his cock.

It was a bigger cock, surely, than anything Vee had devoured in a while, but the wolf took it all admirably as a rush of ecstasy flowed through the bull. He hammered in, rougher and harder, though the wolf kept right on gripping his butt, clenching hard, keeping him where he was wanted. The wolf's need was clear even to him and it was with a bellowing cry and a stomp that almost tipped him off-balance that the bull climaxed.

He'd never had a climax quite like that before, feeling as if it was ripping through his entire body, pulse after devout pulse taking his seed from him. Yet every drop of seed that was spent would be revitalised again in his balls, over and over again: as was the way of a young, virile body.

Hot spurts of cum filled his partner's mouth and even Vee could not stop himself from choking on it a bit, bubbles and drooling rivulets bursting from the corners of his lips. Harvey drew back but only slightly, for the wolf simply wouldn't let him go any further, panting heavily, both of them dragging in as much air as they could to lungs that were too tight with need to think about such a trivial desire. All they could do was stay there, locked in the moment, until every spurt of hot bull seed was spent, poured straight down the wolf's throat as much as was physically possible.

His cock, however, did not soften the moment he was free of the wolf's lips, some part of the transformation pill he'd swallowed keeping it hard and read for action. Vee gasped for breath when they broke, yet there was still a hunger in his eyes that deserved to be sated as he turned around, on the living room carpet, his tail raised and his tight pucker presented.

"Come on, stud…" He groaned, arching his back and bowing his torso down to the ground, showing off his body to the transformed bull. "You know you want to fuck me, want to take me… Fucking show me what that new prick of yours can do!"

"Heh…" Even Harvey's voice was different, panting heavily, raking in deep gulps of air through an open mouth as he dropped solidly to his knees behind the wolf. "You've been waiting for this, haven't you?"

It would have been softer in his usual voice, but Harvey didn't mind that, embodying another persona as he presented his still-hard cock to the wolf's tail hole. All was as it was meant to be as he bore in, slowly, stretching him out around the girth, his paw closing around Vee's cock to make sure his partner was not left out too. He wasn't the sort to forget about Vee, of course; in sex, his partner's pleasure was paramount to his own.

"Unff... Ohhhh... Fuuuck," Vee moaned, dragging out the sounds as his lack of breath stopped him from speaking freely. "Yes... So big... Fucking take me!"

Neither was truly dominant in that moment, though they would certainly have a taste of power play further into the evening. It was all about the rhythm, the pleasure of the moment, every stroke of the bull's cock seeming to drive deeper and deeper, even when the bull's hips glanced off Vee's backside with every thrust. He grunted, a smile trying to twitch to life on his lips, though the moment was right for more, humping and grinding, letting lust rule them both.

There was nothing at all for them to worry about, living and fucking in the moment, though Vee would find himself sore the next day after taking such a big cock. It was all worth it, however, for their mutual pleasure, the delight they shared in rampant sex, moans tangling and intertwining with one another in the air as if they had a life and a mind of their own. Lust was to be shared, after all, and Harvey would not have wanted to take it with anyone other than Vee, driving in deep, his balls bouncing off the wolf's much smaller, furrier ones with every heave of his body.

Vee howled as the bull stroked his cock, jacking him off and forcing him to cum as seed sprayed over the living room floor. Yet they weren't even thinking about that as the bull's thrusts sped up and up once more, hardly even conscious of how long they had been fucking in the slightest. It could have been a few minutes or up to an hour: there simply was no sense of time when Harvey was that lost in the moment.

Yet it was all there for them to take as a rush of ecstasy bubbled up in his stomach, deep within his core, hotter and hotter, churning like a boiling pot on the stove. Yet the bull held his breath for just a few more moments, a few more thrusts, until delight sent him free falling and tumbling over the edge. He bellowed, cumming before his mind had time to catch up with the need of his body, a heady dose of bull seed spurting viscously into the wolf's tail hole, Vee's fluffy tail still sweeping up against Harvey's chest. He panted heavily, raking in what air he could, nostrils flared, so completely lost in the moment that nothing else existed for Harvey but the trembling body of the wolf under him, the thick fur, the rampant grind of Vee's buttocks back against him. Even then, even as he filled his rump with a thick dose of cream, Vee wanted more.

That was just one of many things Harvey loved about him. He gasped for breath, cock spurting, stroking the fur of the wolf's hips and laughing faintly, trying to regain control.

"Agh… Fu-uck… That one…caught me off-guard…"

Vee chuckled and rocked his weight back, showing off just how much he had enjoyed it: as if that could have ever been a question!

It was by no means the last of their lust that night, but, well…there was plenty more to be taken as Harvey showed Vee just what his new body could do.

The two of them most certainly would be found trying out even more full body transformation triggers in the future…

…With "stud-like" transformations being a preference, of course!

# A Dog Kind of Day

*Ugh…*

Alwyn licked his lips, the buzzard anthro lying back on the grassy tussock, though he was nowhere near as relaxed as he should have been. His brown tail feathers fanned out across the ground, though the soil there was well-fed and thick with grass, so there was not a speck of dust on his sleek plumage. His wickedly hooked beak betrayed him as a hawk-like bird of prey, though he had a larger, more impressive wingspan than most native species.

And that could be a pain sometimes too, he thought, resting a lazy hand on his lower stomach, fingers tickling a little lower as they slipped under his T-shirt. The thing was, really…The wings got in the way. His arms were layered with them: wing-arms. A lazy term really, but it was what was in use and that was it. He flexed his hand, the feathers along his arm fanning out a little more, twitching where they could be turned a little as if to angle his arm truly like a wing, controlled by the muscles in his shoulders and across his upper back.

"But not today, hm?"

He wasn't speaking to anyone, not out there, no. He owned the farm, the land on which he was lying on. It was a small endeavour and mostly funded by the holiday cottages that he had converted from one of the old barns on-site. The animals were more or less for show, low maintenance and easy to look after, to the best of his ability. So, Alwyn had plenty of free time on the farm, his fields bordered by a rich birch forest. There had been a weekend cancellation so, oddly enough for him, there was no one else at all on site with him, not one that he had to tend to. Even the fences were fixed, but the weekend labourer did a lot of the heavy work for him, considering the moderate size of the place.

And yet his body, it was not what he wanted. Not then, exhaling softly through the nares on his beak, the slits there that took the place of nostrils. He fanned out his wings to either side of him, stretching his fingertips as far as he could.

Some did not understand why he did not enjoy preening and plucking and teasing his feathers into place but…well…it was Alwyn's story, or not, to tell in that regard. It took so long to oil and shine his feathers, something that non-anthro birds could take the time for, and it was even worse if they ever got waterlogged. As an anthro, he was expected to, of course, shower and make sure he was clean and fresh, especially with the nature of his life and work.

Others had things like fur driers, full body, to help them dry, but feathers just didn't do as well under those, sticking up uncomfortably in weird directions. As dandelion fluff floated over him, carrying a little of the magic of his home and land along with it, the avian parted his beak, heart lifting.

"If only I didn't have to be a bird, just for a little while…"

He smiled as he said that, his beak parted and his eyes glinting. His beak could not form a smile, not really, although that would not be the case for much longer. Not as magic flowed through him, a sense of "otherness" easing into his veins. It was kind of like the strange sensation he got in his arm whenever he got a vaccination, his body acutely aware that something foreign had entered him and adjusting to it. A little tingly, a little awkward, curling his fingers into the feathered palm of his hand and out again.

And yet…that was not quite at all how his body was meant to be, not out there in the sunshine, the deciduous copse of trees to his back, his beak tilted up to the sun. White, fluffy clouds scudded across the sky, but he could not feel the breeze – and neither did he need to, down there and sheltered, soaking up the sunshine. No one was there even to see him naked either, which was another bonus of owning his own property.

"Mmm…"

Alwyn hummed softly to himself, yet it was hard to make the sound, his face cricking and crunching, his beak softening. It melded down, extending a little, but the changes were already upon him and he was pulled through it, a passive player in his own transformation now that the first moments had begun.

For the buzzard anthro could only call on the magic of his home, even if he could not control it. The magic of the land he adored was not his to control, only to ask, occasionally, assistance of. He could not change what had started or halt it at all, only go along with it and see just where the day took him. At least he could choose, in a small way, the species that he transformed into. That was why he had chosen, that day, to shed his feathers for fur.

One by one, his feathers dropped off. And yet his skin was not bare underneath, oh no, a rich coat of black fur smoothing over him, yet it could only be seen when it was revealed. The feathers had to leave him first and Alwyn exhaled a short sigh of relief with every one that dropped away. They were so itchy, so coarse, and he just wanted to rub and scratch at his body. It was the kind of itch, however, that could not be scratched away just like that, as if he had been stung and had a reaction, itching and itching and itching.

"Hmph…"

Alwyn squirmed. It rubbed some feathers off his back, though his attention was not on the feathers that drifted away and disintegrated – only when they were free of his body. It would be okay though, for he would grow a new layer of them when that initial transformation expired. The avian didn't know, however, just how long it would last.

There was one more thing that he didn't expect, his chest shuddering as he tried to take even, slow breaths, filling his lungs with every intake of air. The fur was one thing and yet crawling heat simmered through his body, pooling at his crotch. Alwyn squirmed, his lips parted, beak moulding slowly but surely into them: the longer, chunkier muzzle of a canine gracing his face.

With black fur…hm. He didn't seem quite like a lab, for his fur was too short. Perhaps a Staffordshire Bull Terrier or similar, with the folded over ears. Alwyn's heart surged. That, at least, would be easy to maintain for the span of time that his transformation layered over him, holding him carefully, soothingly, in its grasp.

He would see, yes, in time. Especially as the long feathers of his wings dropped away, despite the greater weight of his body. His bones grew a new heftiness to them, a sense of solidity. Of course, Alwyn could fly as a buzzard, but he did not need to fly when he was more than happy to remain landlocked, his toes flexing and curling.

He had a shirt on and a pair of shorts that came down over his thighs, but his body wasn't growing smaller or larger, even if his shoulders were a little finer. He didn't need, ultimately, as much muscle around his shoulders and across his upper back to support him in flight. Even his abs softened a little and he exhaled as his tongue flattened out, panting lightly. It was a good feeling to let his stomach relax. It did not always have to be contracted and yet his abs and the use of them was just a part of being an anthro bird, their bodies adapting to the needs of their environment.

His beak eased down into pliable flesh and he relished in the sensation of lips, no more feathers left on his body as his head took on a more canine-like shape. His head was not as round as before, his beak protruding as if it had been stuck on, though it still had to become furred. That dark fur, however short it was, prickled and tickled into existence down his muzzle; Alwyn coughed lightly as his nares turned into nostrils, a soft, wet nose taking centre-stage at the end of his muzzle.

Ah, but that heat that he had been forcing from his mind could not be ignored. As an avian, he had typically and traditionally had a cloaca, though his body was set to change. Down there, heat tingled, and he tried to lean into that even more, his body shifting down there to allow less of a hole. For it had to change into a tail hole and an entrance that, traditionally, should only have been for relieving himself, even if it would have many uses when it came to the pleasures of the body.

A cock and balls, however... Yes, those were what he was looking for, the smooth, dark fur coating between his legs too, his crotch flat, but only for a few moments longer. Time itself seemed to slow down as the feathers drifting around him disintegrated, leaving little to no evidence that he had been a buzzard before.

"Oh, yesth..."

It was hard to talk with a changing muzzle, flicking his tongue as it flattened a little further and brushing it tentatively up against his teeth. That was okay though, testing out how he could swallow, though there seemed to be more saliva too in his mouth than usual. It was just something to be aware of as he rested his hand over his crotch, ready to feel everything shifting, flesh bubbling up.

Whereas the rest of his body had experienced a loss, as if he was slimming down into a furred form, his crotch had to grow. A shaft pushed out smoothly, slowly, from the fur, bare and fleshy, though it was a darker red than he would have expected it to be. Again, that was hardly something he could control, grunting and letting out a strangled sound that, honestly, could have been a whine as he desperately tried to grasp at his new shaft.

His new cock just for a while, just until the potion wore off. It would have to be enough for him, for he could not keep a member like that forever, no matter how much that would have pleased him and made his tail wag and wag and wag.

It was better to be a dog than a bird with too many feathers to handle and Alwyn humped up his hips, curling his toes into the ground. There were too many things crowding in all at once, demanding his attention, yet his need dragged to his tail, the drifting, prickling loss of his tail feathers. They had to go, of course, and were truly one of the hardest parts of his body to dry off, though he grunted at their loss as the disconcerting sensation of his spine stretching and lengthening filled his mind. A light crackle rose at the back of his skull, where his spine connected to it, and Alwyn took a moment to take several big, deep breaths to steady himself.

No one had ever said that every aspect of transformation, truly, was comfortable, after all. It was never meant to be easy. That was why those that took the potions he made when the magic of the land allowed him to enjoy a different transformation trigger had to be absolutely committed to the changes. He sold some of them, though only to customers online, so he couldn't be identified.

And, already, Alwyn wanted another canine transformation, something to land lock him, to take him away from the sky. His tail lengthened, beautifully slender and shiny with black fur. He managed a groan that time, a sound that didn't sound like it was meant to come from him – though it was because it was coming from a muzzle, shaping itself softly with lips coming down over his sharp teeth, and not a beak. Everything sounded different with a muzzle and Alwyn was still most used to talking with one. It had been most of his life, after all.

His fingers slowly curled around his cock, even as it thickened to the point where that was not all that easy for him. He didn't have talons on his fingertips to be careful of anymore, but they scrunched back down, cracking like he had split them by raking them over something too rough to handle, into short, stubby claws. Alwyn wouldn't have been able to write, no longer knowing just how to use a pen with claws like that, but that was of no matter to him. He could be careful of where his claws were going while still luxuriating in the moment, the tantalising arousal of change.

"Mmmph... Yes..."

His groan rose more clearly again that time, giving voice more openly to his pleasure. He knew that dogs had knots but he didn't yet know if his transformed body would be given one, working his hand up and down the length of his shaft less than tentatively. Alwyn had been through more than enough transformations, after all, to know how to not hurt himself during them.

The pressure on his bare length was exquisite, like nothing that he could ever have experienced before with a cloaca. He wanted one, craved one, though on him, always, and not inside him. Alwyn tried to instinctively click the edges of his "beak" together but only ended up clacking his teeth, though the same effect was achieved.

"Mmmph... More... Mmm... Come on..."

He grunted more thickly and throatily, feeling the weight in his heels as his taloned feet transformed into paws. Did that mean that his hands were now paws too, in the canine fashion? The pads were slowly plumping up, across the underside of his fingers and the palm of his hands, like most canines had, yet he didn't pay them much mind.

Ah, the terms didn't matter either, he was sure of it. Better to relax into the moment, to enjoy every second of his transformation as the final touches settled over him.

He had left his hips thrust up from the ground as if he was performing a glute raise or a glute bridge in the gym, whatever someone wanted to call the movement, his quads and hamstrings trembling as a little more muscle was added to them. His body, as a bird, had been light and soft, not needing that level of muscle, though just enough muscle so that it could be easily seen and defined through his dark fur was everything that Alwyn could have asked for.

Still, his toes curled down, tipped with the same, stubby claws that his fingers were. The grass tickled his feet, the sensation odd through a coat of fur, yet something that he longed for all the same.

With the final nuances of his transformation settling into place, Alwyn could luxuriate exactly where he was. For the transforming dog, no longer a buzzard, could relax into the moment and feel everything, from the tufty rise of eyebrows along the ridge above his eyes to the wetness of his nose, twitching as he took in fresh scents. His tongue settled more easily into the bottom of his mouth between his teeth and something thick fleshed up against his small finger as he worked his hand up and down his nicely sized cock.

A knot. Just what he wanted.

The dog whimpered, shuddering bodily. It was exposing, to be out there with the sunshine splashing down, though Alwyn could not even bring himself to lie down more comfortably when the muscles that controlled his tail begged him to wag it back and forth, back and forth. He just wanted to keep going and going, letting the pull of muscles at the base of his tail delight him, though his tail seemed to go around in more of a helicopter motion than he had expected.

Ah, well, not every transformation could be perfect!

His pecs swelled a little more, drawing a faint line through the fur on his chest, the skin looser on him than it had been as a bird. If he had spared a moment, he would have been able to move it about lightly by placing a hand flat on his body. But the dog had other more pressing concerns as he grasped his knot with his free hand.

"Oof!"

It was hard to stay up with his legs trembling, his transformation finally complete: a perfect black Labrador that no one would have thought of being anything else. Yet all that was left for Alwyn was for the dog to well and truly enjoy his new form, working his cock over and over, the sound of his hand sliding slickly over his length filling the air along with his needy grunts and whimpers.

All while his tail wagged and wagged, unwilling to stop. His knot was so thick, easily adding another third to the size of his cock, and he squeezed it hard, so close already. It was always like that, when he transformed, but it didn't often press him to get off so quickly. That time was different, however, the canine letting out a strangled howl, not quite knowing how to control his vocal cords yet, as long, hot spurts of semen shot from his cock. They didn't go very far, of course, splattering back down across his lower abdomen, some even dripping back down his cock and adding to the lubrication between his hand and his dick, but Alwyn didn't care.

All he wanted was that thick length spending his load, again and again, making the most of a body that was only temporarily his. And he made sure that he spent every drop from his new, heavy balls, which did not feel at all depleted of cum as he slumped back down to the grass, chest heaving and heart rising.

It was all he wanted… And Alwyn could only be glad, so very grateful, that he was able to take such transformations for his own. Whether he wanted to take on a new life for a while or merely have a dog kind of day, a day where everything was just a little bit lighter for him, well…it was all up to his discretion to go forward as he pleased. And it always would be, all as his tongue lolled over his lips, panting happily.

In the bright sunshine, Alwyn groaned, grasping his cock again, the throbbing knot engorged at the base, and pushed himself beyond the over sensitivity.

Another orgasm with that big, thick knot to tease was just what he needed.

# Tailed Transformation

That was the thing about taking transformation potions: they were so very often unreliable triggers. Sometimes you could pick them up and find they were a dud, that the potion and the magic they had been infused with had faded with the time that they had been available for sale.

Bodie had picked up transformation triggers from all over the place, from coins to potions to even a strange transformation gel that he had smeared on his forearm to activate it. He was pretty innocuous, moving through crowds easily, the kind of guy who wasn't out to cause any trouble – well, except when he wanted to be noticed, of course. That rarely happened, however, with a quiet social group and a good job in a supermarket where he was moving up the ladder. One day, he'd leave there: until then, he'd be more than happy with things as long as he kept going forward.

Yet, in his off-time, Bodie sought more exciting thrills, even when they were the kind of thrills that were contained to his own body. Sometimes, that was all he could hope for, though it was often off-putting when he bought a new trigger and, well, it didn't quite work.

"Hm…"

He'd hoped to swap his bull tail for something a little fluffier on leaving work one evening, glancing up at where the pollution in the sky blocked out his view of the stars. His horns were not all that large, for a bull, but other anthros and people alike gave him a wide birth, for which Bodie was grateful. He didn't want to be bothered on his walk home, even though he had anticipated that the transformation trigger, a small pill that he had swallowed, was going to work within a few minutes.

"Damn thing…" He muttered to himself, his paws shoved into his pockets, even though they were often referred to as "hands" also when an anthro was not a species with specific paws. "Didn't even need to hide out in the bathroom for so long…before leaving…"

Bodie's plan, after all, had been to hide out in the bathroom after getting off his shift at work, leaving the rest of the work after his covered shift to the night stockers, and transform in there. Sure, it would have been a tight fit but, with the transformation he had picked up, it would have been doable. Getting out of there in a new body, however, might have been more challenging. That said, the prominence of so many transformation triggers all around, theft and the like was becoming more and more prominent. A body, however, always left behind something of the original, so DNA was still traceable.

It was fascinating just how far things had come over the years.

Still, that didn't change the bull's position as he grunted and stomped a little, pacing under a streetlight as the pool of light washed over him and then cast him back into shadow. Close to midnight, he had only about another ten minutes to get home.

And then it happened. At the mouth of an alleyway, he paused, head shooting up, Bodie's eyes wide and wild with a glassy sheen to them. He couldn't close his mouth, gargling faintly, the transformation gripping him unrelentingly, even though he had willingly taken the trigger. The bull simply had not been expecting it to snatch him up so ruthlessly – and now that the transformation had taken hold, it wasn't about to let him go until it had worked its full course.

"Unggghhh…"

Bodie groaned, trying to relax, though the need that arced through him was still there, a bundling warmth bristling in his loins. He liked transformation, of course, for more than simply swapping one body for another, need rising, his sheath already trying to plump up and fill out with his aching member. Yet it was merely a by-product to the more immediate pleasure at hand as his skin bubbled and rippled, the short coat of hair all over his body fading.

No... The hair was still there, thickening up – but fading in colour to a soft, pure white that stood out in the darkness of the night. There was no streetlight directly illuminating him at the entrance to the alleyway, though Bodie could only be grateful that there was no one there to see him, words stolen from his tongue as he grunted and moaned. Those were about all the sounds he could make, frozen in place, not even left the ability to shift his wait back and forth from one cloven hoof to the other.

Yet he felt *everything*, from the hardness of the pavement under his hooves to how the cool night air caressed his hide. White fur fluffed up over him, too warm and tickling his nose, and the bull trembled in place, aching to turn his head back and forth. It was an instinctive desire, something that was intended to relieve the tension from the cramping base of his neck, though the weight of his horns seemed less and less.

"Nnngghhh..."

It was a very strange sensation indeed to feel his horns retracting back into his head, his ears pulling up as the skin tugged and pointed into a fresh direction. Although he could twitch his ears, he had never had them be full forward-facing on top of his head, the tips pulling to smooth points, rounded right at the end, dipping into a cup-like interior to better filter sounds. The bull fought the urge to squirm, even though he could not do so, as tiny, fluffy hairs filled the insides of his ears, protecting them.

"Mmmm..."

It was wrong to be transforming out in the open, but, well, Bodie could only be grateful he had not chosen a transformation that was going to greatly change his body type, even if his cock was fully out and harder than ever. It jutted out too obviously against the front of his black trousers, the ones that he usually wore for work in the supermarket, but there was no way for the bull to sweep the heat from his cheeks, tingling and prickling down his neck.

*Ah, to hell with it…*

Any embarrassment would have to be set aside, for it did not belong there, no, not when Bodie was as wrapped up in the lust of transformation as he was. His tail ached and throbbed as his feet tingled, sensing the ground more intimately under his cloven hooves. Yet the bull swallowed a long, drawn-out groan as his tail thickened, fluffing up more and more with that white fur, before splitting.

His cock spurted pre-cum into his underwear as his tail stretched, splitting down the middle with an unnerving, peeling sensation. Bodie gulped, swallowing the saliva that was threatening to pool at the back of his mouth, though he did not even have the liberty of swinging his tail back and forth, no, not even as his transformation progressed.

Oh, but the bull ached to have his hand on his cock, jacking off fervently, biting his lip just to even attempt to keep himself quiet. It was different to any transformation that he had undergone before, from that thick, luxurious coat of white fur layering his body, so cosy even though he would have been happier to experience it nude, to the tails coming. One…two…three… His tail split and split, more fur tickling up against the rest as he tried to curl and twist them back and forth.

Every tail, however, felt like it was connected to the muscle and sinew at the base of his spine and the bull ached to test them out, to see just how much they could be swished back and forth. Yet those kinds of tails were not for wagging but curling and unfurling, letting the eye follow them as they danced a hypnotic sway.

A nine-tailed fox, after all, had more going for it than merely a vulpine muzzle.

"Mmmm…"

The bull's cock twitched and throbbed, but he couldn't do anything about it, not as more and more pre-cum soaked into his underwear. Would it come through the front of his trousers too? Slick cotton clung uncomfortably to the head of his cock and Bodie flinched from it, trying to lick his lips before forgetting that he couldn't do that anymore.

His cloven hooves, however, had to transform too, even if he was already standing as if on the tips of his toes for the digitigrade transformation that he had anticipated on picking up that potion. The hooves melted away as flesh took root from the blood vessels that had already been present in them, a network of his central nervous system that many did not even understand that hooved creatures had.

Yet he felt it, the shape of furry toes forming, the hoof settling down into claws: much shorter and smaller than the cloven hooves he had boasted before. The bull grunted, his tongue twitching within his mouth as if the transformation trigger was releasing its hold on him, though there were still more transformations to come.

His thighs had been bulky and muscular, but a nine-tailed fox with nine, gloriously waving tails did not need that, so they slimmed down, softening the lines of his body under the thick fur so that he was more appealing to the eye in such a form. Everything about him, even under his clothes, spoke of elegance, even if his tails were tucked down against his buttocks, squirming and wriggling against his legs where they tried to find space to grow into. At their full length, each tail would easily be four feet long with a red tip, as if they had been dipped in a rich, oil-based paint.

However, only one could remain outside his trousers at the time, with half of another stuffed through the same gap in the back of his clothes, twitching as if the fluff was going to burst all the way free. The others had to find space and make do with what they had, though even the sensation of the fur rubbing back against his own body was more than Bodie could handle. The bull grunted, eyelids half-closed, yet the final change was still to come, standing on the balls of his feet as they transformed, fully, into strong, flexible paws. It was a good thing, at least, that he had not been wearing shoes, what with having hooves and all!

His face did not swell but collapsed in a little on itself, the sensation of bone crunching and crackling as it retreated decidedly disconcerting. His muzzle stretched a little more, pulling into a more fox-like shape, the soft edges of his snout closing in to a more refined angle. His nose remained soft but tucked up into a red, pointed nose, nostrils hooked as he sucked in a breath, relieved, at least, that his ability to breathe had not been interrupted during the transformation.

That was something and he exhaled softly, finally able to curl and uncurl his fingers, moving his head a little. He still couldn't get his paws down to his crotch, however, where the tent of his cock was still making itself known; that was just something the bull was going to have to deal with in time.

"Oooohhh... Mmmmmmnnnnnngghhhh..."

Bodie didn't think he could last that long, however, as his cock ached and throbbed, the long, smooth length swelling. That was not something the bull had experienced before as the base plumped out, growing into what, from his times in the bedroom with other anthros, he knew to be a vulpine knot. Why was it growing so hard already though? Was that all part of the transformation?

"Unnngghhh…"

He couldn't stop it, but it wasn't up to Bodie to stop it, not as his cock throbbed and pulsed, more and more pre-cum spilling from him as if he was on the brink of orgasm already. The bull shifted his weight, curling his toes, feeling how the short claws tried to dig down into the pavement, but there was still only so much he could do.

He had to ride it out, had to let every ounce of the transformation pull through him. His teeth sharpened, slowly filing themselves down into fangs, for the blunt teeth of a herbivore was not what was needed in his mouth anymore, oh no. A fox could eat meat and, most likely too, even in transformation, would want a carnivorous, omnivorous diet. He practically salivated, coolness swamping his mouth, at the thought of it, though, of course, a bull ate a vegetarian diet normally.

Bodie groaned, trying to hump and rock his hips, though he only managed an inch or perhaps two at any one time. His ears twitched, no longer feeling like a bull but more a fox, his trousers loosening where his tails squirmed and burst over the top of the waistband. With insistent force, they pushed his trousers down, along with his underwear, finally allowing their twisting, white glory out into the dark of the night – where admittedly, they could not be seen as finely as they deserved.

The bull… Well, okay, he wasn't all that much of a bull anymore. Bodie would take his time with them later, however, running his fingers through the soft, luxuriously silky fur again and again, using the claws rising and tucking in from the tips of his fingers to comb through it. Even that was a strange feeling, for he had always had tough, hoof-like tips to his fingers. They were not as dextrous as what some anthros and, of course, humans too had but they had got him by more than well enough in his work and life. The delicate, long fingers looked like something that a pianist may have had and he flexed and curled them wondrously, a soft pant rising from his lips, tickling them as they turned red where black or pink may have been present before.

With a long, elegant fox-like muzzle, he was nearly there, though his cock throbbed furiously. Even though Bodie could not see it, it had darkened to a bright red, drooling viscous pre-cum, the knot hard and aching desperately. Red markings, reminiscent of the fox transformation trigger that had been purchased, of course, danced and spiralled across his head and muzzle, making Bodie wrinkle his nose as they itched and tickled. It was not comfortable but that was just one of many things he actually loved about transformations; they were never meant to be comfortable.

They were meant to be an *experience*, something that had to be taken in the moment, in short pants and grabs of breath, blood rushing to swelling muscles and weight to newly shifting stances. Bodie almost didn't want to think about how hard it would be to walk with paws instead of hooves, but it would all be worth it as he staggered and stumbled home, falling almost more than he managed to walk. Getting the hang of a new body, while needing to be out and about, was a challenge – yet one that Bodie accepted readily.

He always would, just for the thrill of it, his cock aching more and more, blood rushing in his ears, as if someone was playing a drumming, driving beat against his eardrums. He panted heavily, licking his lips, tipping forward a little more, all as it came to a head. His tails thrashed, Bodie's buttocks exposed.

As a nine-tailed fox, he yowled a fox's cry to the less than still night air, hunkering down with his shoulder bumping into the brick wall, need rushing through him. He wasn't even touching his cock and it had all been more than enough to send him free-falling over the edge into transforming lust, his cock throbbing and spurting, sending more cum forth than he ever had thought he'd produced even as a bull. That was strange, very strange, but Bodie was not in his right mind enough to care as his transformation, finally settled over him and Bodie was shocked into movement.

Everything was heavy, so very heavy, forcing him to slump against the wall for some measure of support as he creamed himself into his own underwear, easily soaking through to his trousers. That was by no means going to be comfortable to stagger home with, but the fox was going to have to find a way to get through it, one way or another. There simply wasn't anything else for it as his red lips twitched in a smile and his pale, glowing eyes glinted in the darkness, seeing easily regardless of the low lighting.

"Mmm… Mmmph… Oh…"

It was everything Bodie had wanted when choosing his transformation, though, perhaps, the bull would not have chosen to transform out in the open, his skin prickling with the cool of the night air tickling him. Or maybe it had been that which had added to the experience, the lure of possibly being caught, even though it was late and, truthfully, he didn't think that anyone else would be around.

There was always that chance, however, and he moaned, palming his paw across the front of his trousers, rubbing his still-hard shaft through the too-tough fabric. He wished he had them off, the fox's tails fanning out across his back, but that would have to wait until Bodie was home and free to admire his temporary transformation with the patience it deserved.

"Mmm…"

Panting breathlessly, he smiled more widely, laughing and shaking his head. The sound came out oddly, echoing in the quiet of the night, though there were cars moving down some of the main streets not all that far away. Of course, in a larger town, there was always a sense of movement, that not everyone was sleeping. Hell, he had been in the supermarket covering a shift as the assistant manager only a short time ago, though Bodie would not have usually worked so late.

The lure of tailed transformation, however, had been too much for him and it was with a big grunt that the fox straightened, holding his paws out for balance. It would take him quite some time to get home but, when his transformation lasted longer than even he could have expected, it would all prove to be worth it.

Bodie chuckled as he walked, staggering, trying to hold his trousers up while his tails constantly pushed them out of the way, insistently tugging them down. A long walk home it may have been, but he was the one to reap the spoils.

It was a good thing that calling off work "sick" the next day was a rarity for him…

# Perks of a Shapeshifter

"And how do you think you're going to join me in here? I didn't think you wanted to dive into open water swimming…"

Monte grinned, the grey seal turning over on his back, legs kicking. Sometimes, when the anthro pressed them together, they looked just like a tail, with how swiftly he swam underwater. There was nothing quite like swimming to him, diving into the cool unknown, comfortably opening his eyes whether he was in freshwater or saltwater.

Neither was a problem for him. Or Harlan, to be honest, though the stag had not imparted that information to Monte quite yet. That was just a surprise for him, in the early days of their relationship, the two anthros still very much in the process of getting to know each other.

The red deer smiled and swung his cloven hooves over the side of the riverbank, not minding the soft wetness of the ground seeping into his trousers at all. Harlan didn't tend to notice things like that anymore, considering he so often shed one skin for another, even if he had needed to wait until he came of age to have his first transformation. It happened at different times for every shapeshifter.

The body he had chosen to keep for himself, mostly, was a red deer stag, however, with a tall rack of antlers that fanned out to either side of his head. The tines pointed up softly, though they were not sharp, his fur a richer, redder shade of brown, a small tail tucked up close to his rump. The white flash of fur on the underside of it would have been used, for his species historically, to warn others of danger, though it was not all that often needed for anthros those days.

So, the shapeshifter settled in the form of a stag, down to the cloven hooves and the twitching ears, large and petal-shaped, able to cup and funnel so much sound so he could hear from a greater distance than ever before. His original body, before choosing a stag for the time being, had been a spaniel, a canine with floppy, soft ears. They had not helped him out all that much, though Harlan had always blended into the background before.

There were benefits to blending, for a shapeshifter. But Harlan didn't have to worry about that, no, not at that time. Not with his boyfriend of a couple of months sculling about in the river before him.

"Oh, I spend more time in the water than you know."

Monte blinked up at him, his dark eyes almost woeful, pools into which Harlan could lose himself in. And he so very sorely wanted to lose himself in those pools, even though he would never have drowned in them.

With such a clear and bright day, it would have been a shame for Harlan not to enjoy the water as Monte was, though he had not brought swimming trunks along with him like the seal had. He hadn't known where they were going, so he couldn't have prepared himself. Not that he minded skinny dipping in the slightest either, raising his arms to draw his T-shirt up and over his head.

He'd need a body, however, that was more used to the water. A stag would not do for that and he would be soaked to the skin in no time, not even the lightly insulating layer of hair, which was growing in for his winter coat, along with the fluffier, thicker top layer, enough to protect him. It looked chilly, though the freshness of the day with sunshine filtering in through the trees and dappled shade dancing on the lightly frosty ground was enticing enough as it was.

He wouldn't have traded a day like that, with Monte, for anything.

"So," Monte said with a grin, flipping his tail up and out of the water where it protruded from the base of his spine. "Hm… What are you proposing?"

Harlan took a breath, his chin tipping down, holding himself steady, just for a moment. He had to show Monte, though revealing his shapeshifting side, well… It did not always come easily to him. There had been more than a few negative reactions over the years and then there were the identification issues that came along with being a shapeshifter. That was why they weren't always accepting and, so often, regarding with suspicion too.

"I… I'll show you."

He couldn't go on through something like that, a relationship that was going so well so far, without revealing to Monte who he truly was. No… That was not what a relationship was supposed to be, full of secrets.

He had to be open, sooner or later.

"Harlan, are you okay?"

"Yeah…" The stag took a breath, trying to smile, though it came off a little waterier than he would have liked. "Yeah, I'm fine, it's just…a lot. You'll see."

One way or the other, it all had to come out eventually and he leaned towards the water, his fingers beside his hips, curled into the bank, digging into the softer soil there. It would likely crumble away, a matter of erosion, in the end, but he wasn't focused on that. Not as Harlan drew on his powers to shapeshift, pulling on a form that felt right for the woodland river they were at.

With the peace of the forest around him, birdsong in the air and a buzzard calling in that shrill, keening cry so very high above, it was right. Though Harlan did not reach for the body of an anthro seal with legs and a tail, no, not quite like Monte, though a seal was rather appealing also.

No… He had something better in mind, panting softly as his powers took energy from him.

The first thing to change was his muzzle, needing to soften and fill out a little more, becoming shorter and not quite as refined or as elegant as a deer's snout. He liked that form and there was a sense of loss too from forgetting his deer side, as if he was putting on some new clothes that didn't quite fit – not yet. But they would fit, in time, for it was up to Harlan to make the form fit him.

"Uh…" Monte swam a little closer with a swipe of his powerful tail, effortlessly sliding through the water. "Are you okay? Your face…"

But the seal trailed off, staring, his lower jaw a little slack. Yet Harlan was still aware of him there in the water, keeping level with Harlan with seemingly very little effort, despite the pull of the water trying to sweep him down and along the river.

Harlan could not stop, however, not as his fur changed, his shirt off and only in his trousers, his cloven hooves bare. The red-brown of the deer faded softly to a plain brown, smooth and enticing, the fur laying down close to his body. It did not fluff at all like his deer form, however, and that was something Harlan was going to have to get used to, almost as if it possessed a different weight on his body.

"Harlan…"

He couldn't quite meet the seal's eyes, not even then, not even when he knew he should have, maybe, explained things a little differently to Monte, with words rather than showing. It was too late for any of that, however, and it was not as if explaining with words had got him anywhere in the past either. He hadn't done well with the relationships he had embarked on so far.

But he was young and still hopeful and he wanted to experience what everyone else got to, even if he was a little different from others. That was all he needed, all he wanted, just to be like everyone else.

Still, with his shapeshifting abilities. He didn't want to give a part of himself up just to fit in. But him, as he was, could be normal too.

Harlan focused on his face, how his jaws had to change, his teeth aching deeply as the molars shifted into longer, pointed, carnivorous teeth. It was not a menacing form he was taking on, though some predator anthros could be fearsome indeed, but it was enough, a similar match to Monte that he hoped the seal would like.

"Huff…"

Harlan grunted, working his tongue around the inside of his mouth as it drew back a little, growing lighter and pinker, a little less flexible than it had been before. A deer's tongue was designed for stripping leaves from thorny branches, to take in sustenance from plant matter, whereas the tongue of an otter was for cleaning and grooming, for scooping the contents out of shellfish and for helping devour fresh fish.

He hoped Monte liked otters too. Maybe he would, maybe he wouldn't. Only time would tell.

He had to shrink his height too, growing a little smaller, letting his shoulders become narrower. He, after all, would not need that broadness to him while he was in an otter's form, though he had no intention at all of remaining in it forever. Like many of his other favourite forms, he would keep them for a time and, always, revert to his main preferred one, just so he had a fixed sense of self and identity. At least Harlan's personality never changed when he transformed, which allowed him to remember who he was.

His hooves swung lightly, but they shifted, allowing him more feeling and sensation, hooves melding down into claws while his feet grew. Some called them feet and others called them hind paws: in the end, they were the same thing. His toes stretched with a wrinkling, cracking sensation and he curled them experimentally, testing the limits of his flexibility. Even then, he had to get used to a new body, to let himself sink into it easily, as if it had always been his body.

"Harlan... What are you?"

"I... Uh..."

He tried to talk, though he couldn't quite, not as his jaw shifted, more powerful and able to snap, though it was not as if Harlan was taking on the body of a wolf or anything like that, anything that would need that biting power. The sharp teeth of an otter were designed for fish catching mostly, so were not all that much of a threat. He'd have to be careful, however, more so than usual, when he was going down on the seal...

He blinked up, snatching a quick look at the seal. Monte was still there, close to him but not touching. Harlan shivered, not quite knowing what that meant, losing a little of his height to come down to around five foot six, needing to be shorter than he had been. It felt right for such a form and otters were not traditionally known for being exceptionally lean and lanky.

His tail, however, needed room to grow into and being up on the bank wasn't helping him as much as he wanted. Tipping forward, the transforming otter tried to free it, though his trousers were still in the way. He kicked his legs up briefly, doing his best to squirm out of them, dragging them down over his hips and upper thighs, his underwear coming along with them.

"Heh... You always were one to strip off quickly, you know..."

Monte said softly, pressing in close. The seal rested his hand on the transforming otter's thigh, ignorant to his grunts and huffs, trying to bear through the transformation. It took a lot more energy than many were familiar with, though that wasn't going to change anything, no, not in the grand scheme of things.

"It's okay," the seal said, staying close as Harlan groaned, shuddering bodily, the ache of his teeth resounding through his skull. "I'm here... This... Yeah, wow..."

At least Monte wasn't running or, as it was, swimming away. That was something and, honestly, he had seen that before. He didn't want everything to crumble so quickly and having the warmth of the other mammal so close to him helped a lot.

He blinked, his eyes watery, letting out a gurgling laugh.

"Ah – hic! Ah... Sorry..."

Why was he so flustered? He didn't want to do anything wrong or say anything weird, though Harlan couldn't remember a time where he had been that emotional either.

It would be okay though, he thought, for Monte was there with his big, emotive eyes, watching how desire gleamed in them, a sense of closeness that had not been there before. The seal flicked his tail and Harlan struggled to concentrate, slipping forward and down into the water.

The coolness of the river whooshed over him, enveloping him in a watery embrace, though it was not the kind that would drag him down into the depths of another time. Oh, he knew how dangerous unknown waters were, but he threw caution to the wind with Monte there, the seal knowing the area far better than him.

With his body strong with lean, functional muscle too, he would be more than okay, suited to that environment.

He opened his eyes and peered up through the water. It was not deep enough for him to not be able to stand there, though he waited for a moment, Monte offering him his hand below the surface.

His body changed further, his waist slimming down, better matching his narrower shoulders, fitting his hips too. The pressure of growing smaller was unusual, as if he was being squeezed into that smaller shape, though Harlan never minded it all that much. It would be fine, he was sure, regardless of anything else, for he could always come back up to his preferred size when he was ready, even if it would be nice to be a little smaller and shorter for a while too.

His fur kept him dry under the water, showing off that top layer, which was waterproof. He could dunk himself time after time again, as an otter, and not feel a drop of water touch his skin. Something would have had to be terribly wrong for him to be soaked, genuinely, and he was glad of the insulating layer too.

Still, a warm-blooded mammal thrived on movement, staying warm, and he tested out his muscles, adding a little more to his thighs and calves. He couldn't swim like a deer anymore, which he would have done with kicking and paddling, but had to press his legs together, his tail extending now that it was free to do so. In that way, he curved and undulated back and forth through the water, curving and dancing, pumping his legs and tail together in a butterfly-like kick wherever needed.

And yet there was a greater amount of flexibility to an anthro otter too, something that he could relish in, letting out a laugh with a bubble rising from his lips.

Monte giggled too, taking his hand to draw him back to the surface, their fingers intertwining softly.

"Ah! I didn't know… Harlan, why didn't you tell me?"

Monte gasped for breath, though it was not because he was genuinely out of breath. More, it was the fact he had faced his breath being stripped from him. Harlan clung to him, resting his hind paws on the muddy bottom of the river, a small pebble, smooth from the passage of water flowing over it, making the edges soft and worn. Everything would be worn down over time, even anthros, but Harlan was still growing.

"I… I didn't know what you'd say!"

"Yeah, I guess… Yeah, that makes sense."

Harlan shook his head, yet there was one thing he hadn't paid due attention to. It always made his head throb, but he couldn't be a full otter with antlers rising from his skull, as much as it made his skull ache to retract them – and grow them too, so quickly, in transformation. It was much easier when he went through a shed, but it had been a while since he had purely taken his stag body through the seasons.

Replicating the shed, so no one else would find out he was a shapeshifter, was a fine art in itself, but he grunted and closed his eyes as he focused on his antlers. Slowly but surely, they retracted into his skull, the itching ache grinding, making him feel as if he was pressing his teeth together hard, clenching just to distract himself in the moment.

"Unff…"

"What are you…" Monte leaned in close to him, not knowing what else to do, wanting to help in some way. "Ah, I see… The antlers. Shoot, does it hurt?"

"Yeah… Unff… Yeah, a little."

He shook his head, though the ringing in his ears deepened, the dull pounding aching deeply. It seared through him and he moaned, wanting it to ease off. Yet the tines softened and the bone grew less and less substance, returning energy to his body, though it was not the kind of energy he could use at that time.

Maybe he shouldn't have slipped into the river, naked, at that time…but it was too late to worry about that. He flicked his tail back and forth, balancing himself in the water with the thick rudder.

His fingers too had to grow a soft web between them, stretching from the base, right where the fingers connected to the main part of his hand, but he didn't ask too much of it, no. More weight went to his legs and he kicked back and forth, testing out the force he applied to the restrictive water, his tail hanging down.

The life of the river flowed around him, though he was little of a rock in the middle of it. If not for Monte, he definitely would have been swept away and down the river, even if not very far. It was just tricky to distract his attention between multiple points, when transforming or even when coming to the end point of a transformation.

His teeth settled, feeling more at home in his jaw, and he chuckled softly as he retracted his ears a little too, smoothing out the edges and bringing them in as close to his skull as possible. Everything resounded with a softer sense of ease, his toes curling and then flexing, the tug of the webbing between then reminding him that he was in a new body and had to act just a little differently.

At least Monte was there with one paw on his shoulder and the other on his right hip, supporting him easily. He shook his head, breathing out more comfortably as the antlers, finally, retracted all the way and his fur smoothed over the top.

"Ah… That's better…"

"Mhm… I bet, hon…"

Monte nuzzled him, his wet, whiskered face brushing against Harlan's. Harlan breathed more easily, kicking back and forth under the water, finding a way to settle there, though the river wanted to tug them further and further downstream.

"So..." Harlan took a moment, but only that, to check he was in the form he wanted to be, comfortable and settled, his muscles all as strong as he needed them to be, the webbing between his fingers and toes light for an anthro but just as intended. "Are you mad? I'm sorry I didn't tell you, but... I think you already know why I didn't tell you."

"Yeah, I get it, hon, I just... I was surprised when you suddenly started changing like that!"

Monte chuckled, dropping a kiss on his lips and nuzzling in close, though their tongues brushed, if only for a moment. Heat flared within the otter, pressing in close, though the seal had something more in mind.

"So... Did you change down there too?"

Monte gave him a mischievous grin and Harlan grunted, his smaller ears twitching. There was a lot less ear there for him to control than what he was used to, but that was okay. It was easy to forget something like that as the seal stroked down his body, playing his fingers over to the middle of his crotch and lower still.

"Ah – oh!" The otter blushed, not knowing what else to do. "I didn't think... I just left a sheath down there, and balls too."

"So, all as before..."

His size, however, ended up being a little too big for the body of a lean otter, though it wasn't quite out of place either. The close of the seal's fingers, tender and wicked at the same time, was intoxicating, and he leaned into it with a burbling chirp, which startled even Harlan.

"Ah! That was...ah...weird..."

"Then why don't you float with me a while and I'll see just how well we fit together again..." Monte suggested, nuzzling and nipping at Harlan's neck as he pressed him back to the bank. "Mmmm... I don't know... Why... That shouldn't have turned me on."

"I don't think we have all that much control over what turns us on...or not, hon."

Harlan could say that honestly, after all his experiences in other bodies, things really changed. He'd seen how some looked at him differently with antlers than they did when he had a monitor lizard's leathery hide, for everyone had different tastes. And that was okay too, even if one thing he was not doing was transforming himself to fit those tastes. Harlan only appreciated how those tastes could change with the glimmer of transformation too being taken well in hand.

He arched up against the seal as Monte teased him, palming his cock as he drew him to full hardness. It didn't look at all like the seal had faced any trouble growing hard, though he was bolder, tugging his swim trunks down around his thighs, even underwater, and letting them stretch there, barely clinging on.

"Unff... I can almost feel you inside me," the seal grunted. "You'll still fit, even in this form..."

"I'd be tighter for you though."

Harlan didn't know why he said that, but he wanted it, wanted to try. He grunted, licking his lips, river water sleek over his body, though even the otter knew there was a gleam in his eye. Yes... Yes, he needed something, needed more, lusting and aching.

So, why should he not bottom for once? It just had not been something they had done for a little while, switching back and forth, even though they'd had some amazing sex recently. Turning his back to the seal, he tried his best to flip his tail up out of the way, although bearing it back against the pressure of the water was still a challenge to him.

Like so much else, learning how to navigate that could come in time, if he chose to take a dip with Monte again.

"Unff... Fuck, Harlan..." Monte huffed against the back of his neck, hugging him tightly from behind and pushing his trunks down. "Damn it... You really know what you do to me, don't you?"

The otter smirked, though it came with more of a breathless edge to it than before.

"Yeah... Mmm, only sometimes."

He bucked back, trusting the seal's powerful tail to keep them safe, though it was still a moderately safe stretch of river they were in. He didn't know what lay downstream and the force of it sweeping around them was still enticing, clawing at him, especially as the seal's smooth shaft ground up against his backside.

They both knew what they wanted from the other, though it was trickier to gain when they were in the river, not rooted with any purchase. Yet they could still get it, slowly, as Monte humped and ground up against Harlan's backside, relishing in wet, smooth fur that teased his shaft. Yet it did not float much, still giving the appearance of "clumping" together in that protective, waterproof layer, even under the water, as the seal's soft, grey skin rippled with desire.

"Ah... Monte..."

The otter kicked a little more weakly as the seal pushed into him, finally finding his tail hole in a new form, Harlan's new height throwing him off a little too. It was different, like that, but it was easier to lean into once the seal was inside.

"Unff... Oof... Deeper..."

"Hey, hey…" Monte chuckled, whiskers tickling the back of Harlan's head. "I'm getting there… Ohhh, you are tighter like this!"

Not that Monte would have shunned Harlan in his stag form either, but, well, there were many perks to being with a shapeshifter and it was high time the seal found that out as their relationship deepened.

Not quite that day, however. That day was about the relief of revelations as Monte humped and ground into the otter's tail hole driving deeper and deeper, getting a feel for fucking a different body that was still of the anthro he loved. It was not someone else, not really, but it was something he would have to get used to, all in a little time.

He got the variety, after all, and the spice of life too…

"Mmmph…"

Water swirled around Harlan, yet the otter gave himself over to the deep thrill of being taken, his anal passage clenched so tight around the seal that it was a wonder Monte could thrust at all. But their bodies, truly, were meant for each other, a perfect fit — regardless of the form Harlan took.

That was just how he relaxed into it, his own shaft hard and throbbing, though orgasm was coming to him one way or the other too. He moaned loudly, not caring if anyone heard him, for he had already more than thrown all inhibitions away that day.

He'd never set out to fuck in the river, after all, but if that was what was going to happen he wasn't going to turn it down. Striving to hump back against Monte, the otter quivered deliciously as water swept around him, even that light caress enough for his cock to pulse. Every drop of pre-cum he spent, however, was lost to the water, swept away along the river, even if their bodies would not be.

"Mmm… Oh… You really feel…bigger…ah…like this too!"

Harlan grunted, barely able to talk as he leaned back heavily against Monte. How could his body feel so heavy when the natural buoyancy of the water should have been lifting him? Monte would educate him later (with his cock in his mouth, just for fun) about how saline in saltwater made it more buoyant for swimming, but, well, Harlan wouldn't really care. His shapeshifting abilities more or less kept him safe in situations like that as he could merely add fins or increase whatever he needed to stay alive.

The moment was about lust and lust alone as the seal speared into him, claiming his new tail hole with sharp, needy thrusts. Harlan moaned as Monte took him, though orgasm pulled at his lower abdomen, sinking hot tendrils into his body, twisting and curling, need rising more and more. He hadn't even thought it was possible to get as hard and as needy as he was that quickly, yet every thrust of Monte's simply hit every right spot inside him.

He needed it, grunting and groaning, his tongue trying to flick out and swipe against the side of his muzzle. Gasping, he tried to twist back against the seal, but he was caught there, Monte's clever hand coming around to his front to grasp his cock.

"Mmm… But this feels the same…" Monte breathed, his voice hitching as the seal strove to catch his breath. "You… Mmm… You're going to make me cum so quickly."

"Then do *it*."

Harlan groaned, wanting it more than ever. Maybe it was the relief of Monte still liking him after everything, not shunning him because he was a shapeshifter, or maybe it was something else entirely. One way or the other, it could be explored later as he moaned and bucked into the seal's gasp, the two of them swinging back in close to the bank. Monte chuffed lowly as he pressed the otter over a dip in the bank, where the grassy slope came right down to the water, and Harlan clung to it gratefully.

There, he relinquished all control in a delicious lick of submission to the seal, letting him hammer into him with long, slow thrusts, pushing against the resistance of the water the whole time. Yet that was not enough to stop him from tumbling over the edge into a freefall of orgasm, as if he had been pulled over the lip of a waterfall, orgasm rolling through him, his cock twitching and pulling as semen shot from him. The otter never got to see it, however, as fascinated as he would have been by the ribbon-like tendrils of cum floating through the water, for they simply dissipated too swiftly.

And that was okay too, panting softly and lightly, grunting, letting Monte thrust to completion inside him. Harlan wished he could do more in that moment but everything came along with him and, surely, he would show Monte just how much he appreciated the seal's efforts when they were back on dry land. Until then, he grunted and tucked his chin down against the mud and grass, shuddering as Monte drove in and then let out a sharp, barking, rather seal-like cry.

Finally, he let loose inside the otter's tail hot, hot streaks of cum painting his passage, yet Harlan's mind was already grappling with too many sensations to focus on just one. The absence of feeling hot seed leaking out of his hole, however, was strange to him, for the cool of the river nullified that swiftly. It was something he missed, at least, despite everything.

But they could rest there, recovering themselves, until they had the energy to pull their bodies back on to the bank and lie there, giggling, for another round again. There was time enough for Monte

and Harlan to enjoy one another and the perks of being
a shapeshifter were only just getting started…
In time, Monte would savour every form Harlan
had to offer him.

# Size Lust Transformation

"I've got a surprise for you."

Clay smirked, the red fox sitting back on his partner's sofa, his thick, russet brush flicking around his legs. Wearing only a pair of large boxers, baggy and loose just the way he liked them, the fox was in his element, even though he was ever so slightly putting on an act. Clay was usually confident, preferring to take life by the horns (he'd done that more than a few times with a bull he had messed around with) and not leave anything behind.

He didn't want regrets. Even if that got him into trouble sometimes, Clay didn't care. He did nothing to hurt anyone, of course, and was considerate of those around him. Besides that, he would not hold back because he was scared or worried, for those only told him something was worth doing, worth trying.

No one ever grew and learned, after all, if they stayed inside their comfort zone forever.

That, however, was a little more difficult for his boyfriend, Dario, to manage, the bear's eyebrow raising, the corner of his lips twitching. Even though he was bigger and definitely burlier than the fox, with a soft belly, Dario was the quieter of the two. Maybe, in a way, he sought to make up for the fact that many were intimidated by his height and the broadness of his shoulders, though neither were exactly things the Grizzly bear with his thick, slightly ragged coat of fur could control. He tried to maintain his fur as well as he could though, going for a slick, well-groomed appearance. It never usually lasted until the end of the day, especially when he was still commuting to his office job (a step on the corporate ladder, as it was) via public transport.

"I... Hm... I'm not all that sure I like your surprises," the bear said, affecting a chuckle, though it came a little sluggishly to his lips. "Hm… What did you have in mind, fox?"

Clay grinned and stood, taking in the bear from head to toe. His heart skipped a beat, pounding just a little more swiftly for his partner. He'd chosen well, but it had not felt as if he'd chosen the bear at all, head over heels for Dario before he'd even asked the bear out. No one knew how much he'd agonised over that decision, for it felt like it meant something that time, but he'd always known he was going to do it.

No regrets, after all. Clay had to try.

"Oh, there's nothing to worry about," the fox smirked, licking his lips as he pressed up against the bear's larger body, nuzzling into the thick fur of his neck. "Relax… I just want to make you feel good – and put on a bit of a show for you. Trust me, you're going to love it. Will you sit down?"

Although Dario looked more than a little dubious as to what was going on, the bear still obligingly perched on the sofa and only then, slowly, leaning back against the cushions. He was dressed a little more modestly than the fox, but that was only due to the fact he'd been cooking in the kitchen not all that long ago. One mishap while nude was more than enough for Dario, thank you.

Clay grinned and stepped back, taking a small bottle of pills from the side table in the living room. Although it was a small living area, with the dining table pushed all the way up against the wall (it was not used all that often), it was good for them to both have the privacy of Dario's apartment, free to do with each other exactly as they pleased without worrying about prying eyes. Considering that Clay still shared his apartment with a friend, each of them with their own room, he remained grateful for the luxury.

"Now… Just sit back and enjoy…" He murmured, swaying his hips lightly, pulling every ounce of seduction into his tone, though the velvety roll of his voice came naturally to him. "This is all for you, I want you to get everything out of this…and me."

He chuckled throatily, not giving Dario a chance to ask what the pill was as he downed it, tipping his head back to swallow it down. It slipped down his throat easily (Clay didn't think he had all that much of a gag reflex remaining) and the fox shivered, feeling as if his fur was fluffing up more thickly and standing on end. His hackles tried to raise, but he shivered and rolled his shoulders back, a low hiss easing from his lips.

"Ah…" Clay trembled. "I didn't think it would work that quickly."

Dario went as if to say something and then stilled a moment later, his eyes wide. Clay didn't need to look down at his body to know that it was changing, that the transformation he had been looking for was already in progress, aching and teasing lusciously through his body.

His fur softened, easing back down against his body into a shorter, lighter coat of what could be called hair, if one was using the usual term for it. Horse anthros, after all, rarely considered themselves to have "fur," per se, but Clay had never honestly asked one why that was. It didn't matter, not really, not as he let the denser underlayer of fur fold in close to his body, a little too warm in the living area of Dario's home already.

"Mmm…"

He swept his paws down his chest, the muscle aching and broadening. With less hair on his body, it was easier to see the definition, the red of his fur and the white of his chest and belly shifting, slowly, to a darker brown, like dark chocolate. He shifted his weight and caught Dario's eye with a flirtatious wink, stretching out first his left arm and then his right, rotating each slightly as if he was working out some manner of stiffness or soreness, perhaps in his shoulders.

"Unff… Do you like what you see so far?"

"Yeah…" The bear licked his lips, tipping forward hungrily, though there was a grin trying to pull at his lips too. "I didn't think you'd go for one of the transformation pills… Not even from the sex shop, heh…"

There was a different side of Dario that could come through in sex and Clay loved that too. He had never expected that the bear could be so raunchy and lustful, as if there was a fire burning under his outward appearances, the display he put on for others.

Only Clay got to see that side of him, his muscles thickening and bulking out, defining his round shoulders and prickling down into his deltoids, his triceps and his biceps. He grunted, raising his head, a tremor in his neck simply making him feel it was the right thing to do.

His skull throbbed. That was one of the more difficult parts of transformation to bear through, as his skull shifted into a new shape, drawing on magical energy to form new bone and pull forward a little more. The elegant, softly sly definition of a fox's muzzle would not do for what Clay had in mind and the fox rocked his hips forward with a small whine, blinking as his eyes moved slightly more to the side. The bulge and press of his eyeballs softly, only briefly, bumping up against the inside of his eye sockets as everything shifted was definitely disconcerting.

"Oh, heck… Clay…" The bear groaned, rising while the fox's vision was blurry, though deep lust curled through his tone. "You did this…for me? Heck… You know how much I like…heh…well…stallions…"

Clay panted, trying to work his tongue to speak, but all that emerged from his lips was an embarrassing gargle. He chuckled and tried again, but it only produced the same result, tears in his eyes from holding back the giggles. Dario chuckled with him, running his paws over his shoulders and down his arms, feeling the light tuck of his waist as it swelled a little, giving him a firmer, more powerful body than what he had boasted before.

For the body that was becoming his, however temporarily, was most certainly going to be one to boast about, wide with muscle, his chest broad as it stretched, thighs bulking up as they thickened. It was disconcerting to feel his centre of gravity change, but that was something Clay could get used to more than swiftly enough, if he did all he had planned in such a body.

"Mmmph... Ah..." His tongue thickened, growing fleshier and wider, less able to curl around to the side of his muzzle. "This... Mmm..."

He trembled, arousal pooling in his loins, heat flooding him, from the curl of his toes all the way up to the tightness in his throat. His skull ached still but he managed that as his muzzle grew chunkier, nostrils widening and losing the soft moistness around his nose. Instead, a dark-skinned set of lips grew, wobbling faintly with new flexibility, his teeth biting with a brief snap of pain as they shifted from sharp fangs to a more herbivorous set of teeth.

"Nnggghhh... Ah... That's better..."

It was still difficult to talk but easier with his muzzle fully formed, the skin softening over his snout and his cheek while it curved into a defined, dish-like shape. His ears tugged a little higher, though otherwise did not change position all that much; Clay would have said it felt like they were closer together. It was funny how the little details like that could come through in transformation, even his skin shivering in a decidedly equine fashion. Few species could do that, the skin twitch, and he grunted softly as he tested it out, making his back quiver lightly, just at skin level.

With his eyes positioned a little more to the sides, he was granted a greater range of vision, though there was still a small blind spot right in front of his nose, perhaps where his lips were. He'd find out about that later, surely, though it was not as bad as what non-anthro creatures had to deal with. Even with the tease of transformation, evolution had done many favours for anthros that walked on two legs over the many, many years it had taken place. Clay, however, was gladder for magical progression, what allowed them to live an easy life together and have such fun.

It wouldn't have been possible otherwise. And Clay would never have got to see the hunger in Dario's eyes as he watched him transforming – right into the species that made him weaker at the knees than any other.

"What colour am I?" Clay teased, flicking his tail, though there was a new weight to it that made it want to pull down. "You know all the horse colours."

Dario smirked a little, heat in the bear's cheeks, though Clay only knew of that simply as he knew the bear as well as he did. It was all in the crinkle of Dario's eyes, that hint of shyness coming through even when there was really no need at all for it to be there.

It was just one more little thing he loved about the Grizzly bear.

"A bay…" Dario told him, more boldly running his paws over his body. "There'll be a mane…and your tail is coming in too…"

The transforming fox, even though Clay was not all that much of a vulpine anymore, grunted and twisted, the back of his neck itching as hair prickled to life there in a long, drawn-out pull, as if it was being *stretched* out from his body. His tail, however, was a little easier to bare, the fur softening and growing longer and finer, the bone retracting in it so it only came down a few inches into the dock of the horse's tail. It could still control the tail, but it was more for flicking and swishing than the wag and lift a fox's tail could have shown, all for demonstrating more communication through body language. Anthros didn't tend to use that all that much anymore, however.

That was okay too, especially as he pushed up onto the tips of his toes, the bones in his legs shifting to put him into a digitigrade stance, claws melding into hooves. That was the most challenging part for his balance, gaining a few inches in height while dizziness tugged insistently at him, though the mostly stallion grunted and shook his head, shifting his growing mane from one side of his neck to the other. If he was getting a black mane and tail with a brown body, that must have been what a bay horse was, though Clay would never pretend to be as clued-up on things like that as Dario was.

Stallions had always lured Dario in, but he was intimidated by them. At their university, where they had studied before, there had been a very cliquey, jock-like group of them – or a herd, if he was using silly, technical terms. He'd wanted to get with them but that, well – it didn't really work when he was the kind of bear who wanted to make a connection with someone before having sex. That was all fine and good but none of the horses seemed to want to settle down either and have a relationship, which put them at odds with one another when it came to seeing if anything would work between them.

No one in that scenario was wrong and, honestly, Dario thought it was a little wrong to lust after horses the way he did, almost as if he was fetishising them. He'd still had other relationships too and proved to himself that they weren't the only kind of anthro he could be enticed by, though the preference and enjoyment of them, particularly in porn, remained.

And that was okay too, if Clay was willing to give him what he needed in a rather unconventional way. He knew Dario loved him and not the body he was in, but there was something too about stallions that was going to prove extremely popular with the bear, he was sure.

His hooves solidified and he marvelled briefly at how he could feel the ground under him even through them, not as solid as he had thought they were with a blood flow throughout. His fingers too grew a little thicker at the tips, his nails chunkier, though they still, thankfully, for him, retained a nail-like shape, even if they were deeper and larger, turning a darker shade to match his hooves. Claws were more familiar to the fox, though most anthros filed them down so they didn't get in the way of daily tasks and the general living of one's life.

"Mmm..." He grinned, standing taller and prouder than before, his soft nostrils twitching as he inhaled deeply. "That's better... But I think your favourite part is yet to come..."

Clay tugged down his boxers and let them slide down his legs as he kicked them away, his sheath softening already and widening. It had to be bigger, after all, to contain a larger cock, a cock that would swell and fill it up perfectly, pulling out around his dick as the shaft swelled thicker and thicker.

"Mmm..."

"Oh, fuck, Clay..."

That most certainly had Dario's attention as the bear sank to his knees right there and then, dragging his shirt off quickly and tossing it aside. His trousers would have to wait for a moment, however, as he nuzzled in close to the base of the stallion's sheath, as he transformed, and dragged his tongue up. The fold of flesh caught on his tongue, pulling along with it for a moment, though it was fixed in place and could only be manipulated so far. Under his touch, Clay shuddered, his cock feeling harder than ever.

That was, most likely, purely the effects of the transformation, calling on more blood and energy to make his cock grow larger, adding two and then three and then four inches to the original five-inch length. He hadn't been particularly large, but that hadn't ever been a problem, even if a bigger dick was more inviting under certain circumstances. Dario moaned, taking the head into his mouth as Clay transformed, treating the fox to a unique experience.

Clay huffed, grabbing the bear's head, for he abruptly couldn't bear Dario pulling back, no. He had to keep his mouth there, the soft, wet caress of his tongue sweeping under the head of his cock as he grew into the bear's mouth. The tip flattened out into the mushroom-like head of a horse's cock, even more sensitive than Clay would have imagined, yet there were even more nerve endings in a bigger cock too. His shaft throbbed, giving him the sense that it was twitching and visibly pulsing, though he would have to take some time to find out exactly what a cock like that could do and what was more his mind applying meaning to sensation.

All was fine… It was about uncovering the truth of lust that mattered the most.

The medial ring thickened, defining his shaft, yet Clay didn't get to see it as his dick grew longer and girthier, swelling into Dario's mouth. The bear cradled him gently, sucking him down, even as his throat worked and he swallowed, forced to gulp and angle his head a little more directly just to ensure he could keep taking Clay's cock deeper. It was just a moment, but a little movement like that was more than enough as the horse's aching prick took advantage of the extra space to swell into the bear's throat.

It was difficult for Dario to take a cock like that for the first time but, well, the bear was more than determined to live out his fantasy too. So, he swallowed and gulped, eyes watering, lusting for everything that had been out of his reach for so long. Yet it was his to take, all from Clay, as the stallion grunted and rocked his hips, lips quivering with the hint of a nicker.

"Mmmph… Oh, that feels good…"

His transformation settled around him, the final details pulling neatly into place.

The tease of the muscles at the base of his ears, allowing him to better control them.

An ache under his tongue where the sensitive flesh pooled in the base of his mouth.

The sway of his tail as he tested the limit of it, swishing it back and forth, pulled down under the weight of the long, black hairs.

Even his balls too, losing their fur and becoming dark-skinned and hairless, exposed in a velvety sack.

They fattened up, swelling to fill the space given to them too, his new body seemingly keen to make use of all it could, even if that was partly his mind trying to make sense of sensations. As they both explored more transformations together, they would find out more still about what made transforming so erotic and, of course, how it affected the brain too.

But not that evening, no, for that was their first time using the transformation pills, even if it most certainly would not be the last.

Standing firm on his hooves, the stallion hunched over the bear, needing to steady himself on his head, fingers stroking behind his ears. It was not entirely a natural position for him, though it was just a little easier when he braced his legs and flexed his hocks. There were so many details of his transformation he simply had not had the time to consider as yet, but those would have to wait.

The succulent sweep of the bear's tongue under his cock was too intoxicating to ignore, Clay panting, drunk on arousal. He'd never thought every throb and pulse of his dick could come with such a physical pull to it, spilling pre-cum as the bear eagerly took it down his throat. As far as the transformed horse could see, not a drop escaped the corners of the bear's dark lips and he shuddered bodily, his tail flicking back and forth. Even then, his body strained to convey those outward expressions of excitement, need clawing at him.

"Unff… Dario…"

He groaned, shaking his head, the shift of his mane catching him off guard in a flickering tickle of sensation.

"It's…ah…so sensitive…"

But he didn't ask Dario to stop, no, not when the bear was finally getting everything he could ever have wanted in the best way possible. Dario moaned around him, soft vibrations travelling from his mouth into the stallion's dick, and bobbed his head back and forth, working his maw over the full length and using his throat. Even though he'd been with Clay for quite some time, at least over a year by that point, he hadn't been with many very large partners before. In life and love, they had differed in terms of experience, with Clay having more sexual partners than the bear.

Yet they didn't have to be the same and they complemented one another, Clay groaning as he humped languidly into the bear's muzzle. Despite the sense of need and urgency inside him, swirling deep and pushing him to thrust, he did not take Dario's muzzle more roughly, not wanting that for the moment. No… It was all about allowing the bear to savour every last moment of his transformed body, although it had to be said too that the horse was most certainly getting a lot out of the deal too!

It was something he would have been very keen to do over and over again as Dario slavered over his cock, his paws coming up, pressing to his inner thighs and then reverently cupping his balls. As if he was worshipping him, the bear caressed his nuts softly, rolling them back and forth between his paws, letting them rest on the dark pads, careful of his own short claws.

"Mmmph…"

Dario groaned around him and the stallion whinnied, surprising even himself with the shrill sound. He wanted to cum so very badly and it did not at all feel as if he was going to be able to hold back. The drive was there, the need to cum, and his lips wobbled softly, nostrils twitching, even his balls feeling as if there was a deeply seated ache present there – such that could only be relinquished in spending his pleasure.

"Unff… Gonna…cum…" He tried his best to warn Dario, though the bear did not pull back from his cock in the slightest. "If you…ah…mmm…so good… Keep doing that…"

Dario did not stop, however; if anything, the bear worshipped his dick even more ardently, the rise and fall of his muzzle on that mighty spire increasing in pace while the stallion thrust. He couldn't help himself, though he couldn't believe just how well the bear was devouring his cock too, sinking deeper and deeper, as if he was trying to get his nose all the way to the base. It was, however, a rather long cock and that would take a little time and practise for the bear to get the hang of – and perhaps some more transformation pills too, for multiple sessions.

Something for them *both* to look forward to.

"Mmmph... Nnngghhh..."

The stallion groaned, stiffening suddenly, his black tail flagging behind him as it pushed up. Yet not even Clay could have prepared for the deluge of cum leaving him, a neigh breaking his lips in a startled cry, awash in ecstasy. Pump after pump of semen flooded his partner's mouth and throat, causing him to cough and choke lightly, though he was able to draw back just enough to catch his breath again. Not much was going to stop Dario, after all, from sucking down every last drop of cum from that hot length that he so sorely needed, seed spilling from the corners of his lips and dribbling down his chin and chest.

"Mmmph!"

Clay tried to withdraw, but the bear held him fast, his paws on the backs of his thighs, locking him in place. Even when he tried to relieve Dario, just for a moment, the option was taken from him, though it was not all that bad when he gave the bear everything he wanted.

Right up to the point where every last spurt of cum had left him, his cock still hard. Clay licked his lips, rubbing the bear's head and behind his ears, though he was still a little worried at the fact that his cock had not softened at all. Ultimately, it seemed harder still as he withdrew it from Dario's mouth in a pop of splattering, gleaming cum, the head thick and flared wide. Even Clay was impressed that the bear had taken that down his throat as it was.

"Mmm, Dario… You really like this, don't you?"

Perhaps the horse had not realised quite how much before, though there was no shyness in Dario anymore, not as he leaned in and ran his tongue, tantalisingly, from the base of that devout shaft to the very tip.

"Mmm… Lie back on the sofa for me…" He moaned, phrasing it as neither a request nor an order. "I want…to ride you."

Clay smiled and softly did as the bear wanted, moving slowly and fluidly. It was not only him trying to get a feel for his new body, how he had to walk a little differently "up on his toes," but also him trying not to break the spell for Dario. He didn't want to pull the Grizzly out of the lustfully trance-like state he was in and lay down for him, his cock jutting up still, hard and throbbing with need.

It felt like he hadn't cum at all as the bear stripped himself full and, nude but for his brown fur, straddled him, facing Clay. His thighs closed around the horse's hips, but he had to raise himself high to get the bouncing, tingling head of the stallion's dick pressed up to his tail hole.

Clay nickered softly, a bubble of pre-cum helping to lubricate the bear's tail hole, soft and yielding, though he didn't think that was going to be necessary. They could take it as slow as they wanted. And perhaps he would even stay hard through orgasm, again, allowing him to give the bear even more.

The stallion hoped so, positioning his cock carefully with his paw as Dario sank on to it, stretching around the wide head and moaning aloud.

"Oh, fuck…"

"Take it easy..." Clay murmured. "You look amazing..."

In such a position with the bear on top, riding him, he was able to drink in the Grizzly's body, everything he adored about him. For it was Dario who made it special, more so than anyone else he'd been with, struggling to take him at first and then finding a rhythm and a pace that suited him. He bucked and ground into the horse's lap as if it was the last fuck he was ever going to get, something raunchy and randy breaking through in a new side to the bear.

His grunts caught the stallion's attention and Clay moaned along with him, aching to be there. He would never have not wanted to be a part of such a hot, intimate experience with his partner, but everything worked out just the way it was supposed to. More than used to having sex with his boyfriend, the stallion didn't think he could get anything more out of it from simply having a different cock, but even that was set to surprise him.

The glands were so sensitive that he relished in every clench of the bear's backside, muscles tightening around him in ways he would never have thought possible, not before. Dario sank down, using every inch of his cock, though the bear's eyes were always on Clay, meeting his.

Even in satisfying his fetish, he saw Clay for who he really was and the stallion covered Dario's paw with his own where it landed on his chest, over his heart.

"Unff... I'm gonna...cum quick..." The bear moaned. "I...didn't think...oof..."

The horse would never find out about what Dario "didn't think" but that was okay too. All was as it was meant to be as he let the bear ride him, taking his cock in short, needy dips of his body, almost reluctant to rise again even as he bounced on the stallion's lap.

Every pull of his ass around Clay's cock too brought the stallion closer and closer to orgasm, huffing and panting, his lips parted for the delight of more.

Together, they raced for climax, even though there was no urgency behind it. The bear's cock bounced before him, no paws touching it, the long, fleshy spire aching for delight. It was a couple of inches bigger than what Clay's cock was naturally, but the stallion kept his eyes fixed on it as they arced closer and closer to orgasm.

For, when it came, that jetting-off of cum from Dario's prick was what set him off too. He'd never seen such an alluring, inviting sight as the bear grunted thickly, deep in the back of his throat, and suddenly hunched down over his partner, shoulders rounding and juddering. It was all Dario could do, clearly, to bear through the enormity of his climax, painting the stallion's lower abdomen in his seed, even streaking up to his belly.

The stallion lost control, thrusting up, scrabbling against the sofa for purchase as orgasm claimed him too. Long, hot jets of cum shot up inside his partner, painting his tight passage in a creamy deluge, slickening back down the length of his cock. Yet that lubrication was very much unneeded in a moment like that as he moaned and shifted his weight, trembling at the height of climax. Wave after wave of pleasure crashed through him and, together, Clay and Dario rode out their orgasms exactly as they were meant to.

When they came down, of course, there would be a mess to clean up – a rather big mess, in fact. But that was something, like everything else, they would tackle together, growing closer and closer, the bear and the stallion finding new ways to love one another. Especially after the fox de-transformed, all the way back to his regular vulpine form.

Whatever form he was in, Dario would always love him. Even if he lusted for something in bed, exploring different kinks and body types to the benefit of both…

# Size Gain

Mica groaned, the lion's tail flicking back and forth, pressing his lips together. The feline, however, was not truly upset about losing the game show round, even if there had been a big cash prize.

No one entered the transformation game show, where wild and crazy transformations – what others can come up with as "punishments" for every lost round – are the norm, for the money alone. They joined because they wanted it, because they longed to feel the tug and the pull of their skin shifting and shivering, bloating out with new flesh or even their muscles pumping up to extreme proportions.

He had wanted to win, however, so he could bulk up and enjoy a few days of being heavily muscled, imbued with physical power. The game show stage stretched out before him, a hungry crowd clustered in the darkness beyond the lights, though he was used to that. Even though Mica had more often than not been a viewer to the transformation game show, he had never been up on stage.

And that was better than ever, standing opposite the winner: Cliff. The thing was, it was the winner who got to decide what temporary transformation they placed on the loser of the final round. From the looks of the stoat, his tail flicking back and forth and his lips stretched into such a wide grin that he almost looked rattish in his appearance, he had something very special in mind for the lion.

"Be kind to me," Mica said, offering the stoat a sheepish grin. "This is my first time…you know?"

"What?" Cliff cocked his head, though that cheeky grin remained the same, hypnotising and inviting. "First time…like ever?"

The lion scoffed and combed his mane back from his face with his fingers: a nervous tick.

"No… Just being in the transformation game."

There were rules, of course, as to what transformations could be placed upon contestants, so nothing permanent or disfiguring would be utilised unless express permission was given for the latter. Mica too had noted down his preferences in the intake forms. It was just up for debate whether the stoat would take advantage of those.

With the roar of the crowd in his ears, everyone waiting to see what the loser would be transformed into, he took a breath. Cliff snapped his fingers with a short, sharp, decisive nod, setting off the transformation.

It happened quickly, a flash of light leaping from the magic holder handling the transformations, though his eyes weren't on them, no, not by any means. They remained fixed on the stoat even as his back shot ramrod straight, a jolt like electricity shooting through him.

"Oh…"

The lion could not help but moan, warmth flooding him. It was so soft, pooling and flowing through him like a liquid, though he hadn't been struck by magic for a very long time. His fingers twitched and he held them out before him, his paws soft on the underside with a pad.

And yet it was not Mica's paws that changed first, even though that was where all his attention was focused, no. His tail trembled and he stiffened a little more, the lash to it softening, falling down, all as it shrank up and up and up, retracting into his body.

The lion shivered.

"Ohhhh…"

Oh, that felt weird, very unusual, but not bad, more as if his spine was being shortened, compressed a little as it sank back up into his body. Yet a few inches remained as the fur slipped away, not to be absorbed or disintegrated or anything really, as a long spill of black hair fell from it.

It could only be seen as one thing – and that was a horse's tail. The lion groaned as he wiggled his tail back and forth, the lack of flexibility unnerving, for he was used to a much longer tail that he could curl and twitch. That one was shorter, but it did play the hairs against the back of his legs nicely, sweeping back and forth.

He didn't lose the fur on his body, though it darkened, as if an ink blot was spreading through him, turning his fur black from head to toe. It became shorter and denser, laying down flat to his body so his muscles were shown off a little better, though Mica had only been moderately muscled – nothing overly so.

"Unff…"

He shook his head as his muzzle pushed out, his sharp teeth retracting with a dull ache, his tongue thickening up within his muzzle, a little wider than before. His nostrils pulled up into a soft curve, fluttering with every breath, and his lips grew a little plumper and more velvety.

"Mmmph…"

The lion grunted, trying to work both his tongue and his lips together, his tail flicking back and forth with that long, inviting spill of hair. Though his teeth retracting and filling out took up more space in his mouth, his jaws longer with a gap in his teeth. That was the small space at the corner of an equine's lips, where there was a gap between two teeth on each side, but it still felt odd, his tongue going back to that spot, again and again, trying to make sense of it.

Still, his body layered with muscle – muscle that Mica would never have dreamed of having on his regular old body. His chest broadened, his pectoral muscles fattening up, rising to show much greater shape and definition, his shoulders rounding out smoothly.

"Mmm…"

"Hey, you look great like that, stud…"

Cliff chuckled, winking at him, though Mica could not even blush. His short coat of hair, not quite fur, would have hidden any heat in his cheeks anyway, a white stripe dipping down the front of his face. His ears twitched, softening into more petal-like shapes as they folded together to the base, the tips pulling into tapered yet rounded points, losing the feline smoothness and easily recognisable shape.

It didn't have to be there, even as his thighs thickened, swelling into tree-trunk legs, the point of his quad tapering a little as it came down to his knee. He'd never had calves like that either as his clothes strained around him, his jeans not really suited to transforming. Mica had wanted to be modest, however, even as he grew and the seams of his jeans strained around his thighs, tight around the crotch.

*Ah… Damn it…*

The stoat eyed him up, grinning as he took off his shirt and let his shorts slip down a little, revealing the top of his sheath, the pink of his cock protruding— just a little.

"You're going to want to be rid of those clothes soon too," he advised. "But…you could just let your body rip them too."

Mica panted, wanting to ask what the stoat had told them to do for him – but he couldn't find either the breath or the words. Not even as his jeans ripped between the legs and up between his buttocks, heat rushing to his face and crawling down his neck as it lengthened a little, the vertebrae of his neck crackling faintly as they pulled into a longer, equine shape.

Yet his body could not hold itself within his clothes as he gained height, pushing up on to his toes. Thankfully, the transforming lion had not been wearing anything on his hind paws, though it was fascinating, even to him, how his nails lengthened, pushing up so he was standing on them, forming a hard shell of a hoof instead, complete with the softer, triangle-shape on the sole. He had known what that was called once upon a time, but the name eluded him in the moment.

The stoat's hungry eyes on him settled him a little, though Mica was not all that concerned about his body being on show to the crowd. It was what he had signed up for, even though he was ever so slightly shy, pulling back as his shirt strained across his chest, biting into his underarms until it too was forced to rip.

It tore and he clawed at it with a roll of his eyes, his height resting at something like seven feet tall. Mica wasn't about to ask someone to measure him, not when heat curled in the pit of his belly, need rising. Transformation, after all, was erotically enticing for him, his cock trying to plump up even then, despite his body using as much available energy as it could to sustain the changes.

"I'm going to enjoy you so much…" Cliff said, his voice low and sultry, cutting through the crowd and the cheers, even the game show announcer. "Mmm… Is that okay? You up for that?"

Mica trembled but still managed a weak grin.

"Hell yeah, I'm up for it," he confirmed, not wanting to leave any doubt or regrets on the table. "Mmm… Fuck… My clothes…"

"Here, I'll help."

Mica let the stoat do as he willed, cutting and ripping the rest of his clothes from his body, though the transforming lion-stallion (who looked more horse than cat) squirmed a little when Cliff got to his underwear.

That was ever so slightly embarrassing and revealing but it would soon be swept away in the majesty of his body, his mane slipping back to the reverse side of his neck to fold into the sensual fall of a horse's mane.

So… He was no longer a lion but a stallion, the minor notes of his transformation settling into place, his heart pounding mightily. Even his organs had to keep pace with his increased size, filling his ribcage with his heart and lungs, the bellows expanding mightily as he inhaled. His guts gurgled – which was perhaps the most embarrassing of all as the stallion stood tall and proud with a long, flowing mane and a shy smirk on his lips.

Well, Mica couldn't be shy forever, after all, standing nude and proud as his sheath folded down, the soft skin darkening. His balls grew fatter, hanging down a little lower, though, to his eye, he wasn't expecting anything huge to change there.

As he was rendered nude, the stoat respectfully gave him just a little more space, so he wasn't hanging all over him, though Cliff's desire was evident. The stoat's cock swelled and he pushed his shorts down again, sliding them off his thighs with his shaft swollen, though it did not quite yet seem fully hard. That would come in time, though not much time as he took in the horse's studly body, firm with muscle, his waist tucked in slightly, pointing down in an upside-down V-shape to his hips. The bones of his hips showed through faintly, his glutes firm and muscled, tensing as he tested his balance on hooves rather than paws, rocking back and forth.

"You got to get used to that," Cliff said, eyes alight, his tail swinging softly behind him. "The weight shift… You're going to love the next bit so much."

Not quite understanding what he meant, Mica trembled, grunting as his sheath tingled.

"Oof…"

As Clifford chuckled, the taller stoat enjoying the show, Mica's body ached, pooling in his crotch. He didn't just seem to be a horse, no, but…something was happening to his cock too.

"Oof… What have you… Nngghhh…" He groaned. "I… What did you *do*?"

The stoat smirked, the tip of his tail twitching.

"Oh, just a little something I found in your search history," he said with a wicked grin that he just couldn't keep from his lips. "You really shouldn't leave your phone hanging around places like this."

Mica's cheeks burned as his stomach lurched, yet that didn't do anything to steal the heat pooling in his crotch. The soft fold of his sheath plumped out, filling out…and grew.

"Ohhhhh…"

The transformed horse could not help but moan, though he was about to become the stallion of all stallions as his cock filled out, bloating out from his sheath as it swelled. But it was not the normal swell of a cock pumping full of blood and growing to full hardness, no. It was bigger than that, the previously smooth length rising with a medial ring, adding inches to his previously moderate six-inch length.

He squirmed, aware of the cameras trained on him, that everything was being recorded, that it was all turning into a sex show, his cock easily showing through his ripped clothes. There was no way for him to hide it even as Cliff joined him up close and personal, running his paws down the stallion's chest with an appreciative murmur.

"Oh, you look so good like this… Who would have known our kinks would match up so well?"

Mica grunted, trying to shake his head, though all his energy seemed to have been concentrated in his nuts, the already fat orbs filling out more and more and more. The skin stretched, letting them hang down a little lower, though there had to be space for them to grow into, one way or another.

"Uh… What…" He struggled to push the words out, his tongue feeling thick and fat in his mouth, as if it had become more unwieldy. "You… What do you mean?"

"Because I'm into this too," the stoat said, a grin on his lips. "Do you mind? Can I touch you?"

The horse warmed through. It was good to be asked permission, even though they had already signed forms and whatnot concerning their permissions for the game. But it was that note of respect that had him blushing and whimpering a bit, not even sure what he was doing – but wanting more all the same.

"Ah – yeah… Yeah, you can…"

His cock swelled, growing increasingly, far beyond the size it should have been if he had been just a regular equine. He was taller than any stallion he'd seen and the girth of his cock would not have fit inside any regular anthro…but transformation could be applied to bodies in more than outward appearances.

The stoat moaned, gripping the stallion's cock, no longer able to get both his paws around it at once. Yet all Mica could do was relish in the pleasure as his cock grew out past two feet long and kept going, fatter and thicker around like a one-litre bottle of soda.

"Mmmph… Oh…"

"Yeah, just hang on in there, stud," Cliff encouraged him, massaging down the full length of Mica's cock with both paws. "Wow, you look so fucking hot like this…"

Mica wanted to thank him for the praise, but things were moving too quickly for that as the length of his cock filled out, the head flaring thickly, flat and throbbing. With every pulse of transformation-filled blood into his cock, the head twitched, a dollop of thick pre-cum sliding from it. Even the slit in the tip was obvious as his cock grew out past the height of the stoat's head, four feet long and still growing, but Cliff was too busy pulling that cock down to meet his lips.

"Mmm…"

Cliff groaned as he tried to take the fat head of the stallion's dick into his mouth, though he couldn't get his lips all the way around it, no matter how much he tried. Or, at least, that was what it seemed like at first as his jaws parted more and more widely, his body rendered much more flexible because of the transformations that he'd asked to be applied to him too. And that was exactly how he took the stallion's cock into his mouth, his jaws opening impossibly wide – and yet there was nothing grotesque about it, a smooth, natural, lustful slide.

The horse tipped forward, shoulders hunching and rounding as if he was trying to manage the sensations running through his body, everything from the twitch and clench of muscles to the rock of his hips and blood rushing to his cock. For there was a lot more cock to swell out without delay, inflating massively, stretching out the stoat's throat and maw more. Oh, but it all had to go somewhere as it burrowed down into Cliff's stomach, pre-cum sloshing into his belly, pump after pump.

Mica moaned, shuddering in place, though he could not pull out, no. His body wouldn't let him, not when the stoat was gripping his thighs like that, as if he could hold the stallion there if only he tried hard enough. Cliff grunted around his dick and, even then, he could feel the soft vibrations and tremors from his lips fluttering against his cock. It was strange that such a small sensation could be felt just like that and he marvelled at it, his nostrils flaring sharply as he inhaled a big puff of breath.

"Oh... Oh, Cliff..."

The game show announcer was saying something, yet it rose through the din and clamour of the ground and their lust as if it didn't matter. It may as well have been just the two of them there, regardless of being recorded and photographed, the stoat sucking down inch after delectable meaty inch of the stallion's swollen cock.

His dick must have topped out at around six feet long, not so long that it would have been taller than him if it had been put upright alongside Mica's new body. It was only temporary and yet the swollen spill of his balls hanging between his thighs inflated next, the skin pulling and stretching, the strain of it growing to encase his new nuts tingling through him.

The stallion grunted. That wasn't a feeling he was expecting, panting softly, licking his lips, trying to find the stoat's head, though Clifford was still out of his reach, so he couldn't even comb his fingers through the fur around his ears and the back of his neck. It separated them a little and Mica didn't like that.

Even though the lure of having a massive cock, his body out of his control with his permission, bloated through him, Mica's tail swinging lazily as he stood taller, his paws resting on the base of his cock.

"Ah... Fuck, Cliff..." He muttered under his breath, catching the twitch of the stoat's ears. "I want to fuck you so badly right now."

Cliff's tail flicked up, but Mica didn't know what that meant. That was the only thing with sucking cock: communication was rendered just a bit more difficult with that. But it was a challenge he was more than willing to overcome as every throb of his cock sent another thick spurt of pre-cum into the stoat's belly.

Even that part of Cliff, after all, could not help but swell to accommodate Mica's cock. Even pre-cum had to go somewhere and it pooled heavily in the stoat's stomach, filling it up and making it sag down under the weight of all the excess, viscous fluid in there. It bloated out and out, even though Mica's swollen dick had to be pushing into it too, the overfilling of cum making his belly bloat out and forwards, despite the weight pulling it down. At least there were never any silly side effects to transformation in the transformation games!

But Mica needed more, so much more, even as he lusted for the sight of the stoat down on his knees, almost turning into a fetish object as much as the stallion was in that moment. Things just came about like that, though the trembling of Cliff's belly had a simmering heat to it too – especially with every further throb of pre-cum sloshing into it, splashing up against the strained inner walls of Cliff's stomach. Every moment slowed down and dragged out and the horse smirked faintly as Cliff rolled his eyes back, locking his gaze with the horse's.

Fuck. That was hot too, extremely so. Who knew eye contact during sex could be that intoxicating? The stallion's breath hitched and he grunted deeply, gutturally, tail lashing the air.

More, he needed more… And he was going to have it too.

"Stay there."

He held up his paw too, with the palm facing out, to make sure Cliff was clear on what he was being asked to do, though the stoat seemed only too happy to follow Mica's lead in the moment. It was harder, however, for the stallion to shuffle backwards, still in the process of getting to grips with his new body, scraping his hooves over the stage as he dragged his cock from Cliff's mouth and throat. The long slide was almost as torturously pleasurable as penetrating the stoat in the first place, wet heat clinging to his cock, the flare dragging through Cliff's throat.

His balls, however, still grew, the transformation nearly fully complete, though they could have perhaps taken their time a little more so the cameras could have caught his balls inflating. Yet the overflowing slosh of cum within them needed to fill every iota of space they were allowed as the overfilled balls bloated past his knees and lower still, so big that he couldn't even imagine ever emptying them fully. Maybe that was not the point. Yet it did not matter, could not matter, not as he grunted and rocked his hips, need coursing through him, electric and tingling, a current of longing running through him.

When the flare finally popped free of Cliff's mouth, Mica nickered, another thick spray of pre-cum jetting from him, as if he was already cumming. But he couldn't, not yet, for he only had one place he wanted his cum to go – and that was inside the stoat. Just not down his throat, which was why he had pulled out in the first place.

"Can you turn around?" Mica said, ears twitching, unable to keep the smile off his lips. "If you think you can take this cock you gave me up your ass, that is…"

Cliff grunted his approval, though it was tricky for him to crawl around on all fours, his belly keeping him down even as the inflated stoat's stomach dragged across the stage. A slick sheen of pre-cum on the stage rendered it slipperier than it should have been too, but he managed it, pushing his tail awkwardly off to the side as Mica lined up with him.

And then he pushed inside, a camera zooming in on the point of penetration as the transformed, stretchy stoat pulled around the stallion's huge cock. It was a cock that should never have fit into any anthro in the whole world, regardless of their size, but the magic of transformation went a long way. So it was that they got to enjoy fantasies and fetishes, safely, in reality too as he drove in, the tight grip of the stoat's tail hole almost enough to send him over the edge.

"Unff... Ah..."

But he had to keep going and he had to hold off a little more, so he could best enjoy the moment while it was there for him. It would not last forever, after all, and he reached forward, straining, the deeper he went, to grip the stoat's hips, wanting to drag him back on his cock.

He had to jam his shaft savagely into Cliff's hole, however, before he could get there, the strange elasticity of the stoat's tail hole intoxicating. Oh, it was a sensation he could get drunk on, losing himself there. Though, like with all transformations, he'd have himself to go back to and find when the time came too.

Knowing that it wasn't permanent was tricky too, a sense of impending loss pulling at him. But he couldn't let that demand further attention in that moment, not as he pressed on, rolling his hips forward slowly and smoothly. The friction dragging down the length of his cock took up every bit of his attention and he panted lightly, licking his lips, even if there was only one way to release the tension in his body.

Oh, but the explosion of orgasm was coming, eventually. It rumbled deep within his balls, finally transformed fully and resting on the ground, though they were not so large that they stopped him from standing on his own two hooves. Mica was glad of that, even then, but he wouldn't have minded seeing if they could go even larger in another transformation too. Perhaps he would have to play the game show again?

Ah, but that was for another time as he thrust and tried to find his footing again, grinding into the stoat's tail hole as the pucker clenched around him. It was the tightest point as he grunted and shuffled in closer still, stuffing Cliff with every inch of his cock he dared. Would going too far hurt Cliff? Yet the stoat's mouth was open in a long, low drawn-out moan...

"Ohhhh..." Cliff groaned, tongue pressing out briefly over his lower lip. "I want... Ohhhh..."

But he couldn't even vocalise what he wanted when he was getting it – every drop. Pre-cum pumped into him from his backdoor entrance as the horse thrust with his grossly inflated, hyper cock. Cliff moaned as he was speared into, yet his body easily stretched around the length, taking everything Mica had to offer, though it had to be said the horse was holding back ever so slightly.

He'd have to build his confidence for another time, for not everything could be gained in a day, despite his size. And that was okay too as that hot, wanton hole clenched and squeezed around him, the stretch making it feel as if the stoat's body was pulling around him, milking him of his load.

"Unff... Gonna make me..." He trembled, his tail shivering, flagging up a little higher with every moment. "Cum... Ah..."

Yet he still strained to savour it, even as the stoat weakly howled and bucked on his cock, arching and bucking through his own orgasm. He turned his head back and forth, tongue hanging out, yet it was up to Cliff to bear through it, to languish there where he was on the precipice. He could have held that for longer, if he chose to, but his need was so great that he gulped and heaved, licking his lips, pleasurable ripples running down his cock, milking his length.

His balls ached fiercely, cum sloshing and churning inside. Oh, but how he needed to cum, rolling his hips, the pulse and clench around his girth driving him mad. His tail twitched, pushed up as high as it could go, as if he was proudly flagging and striving to show off his assets even then. Mica's balls, of course, were evidently on show as they hung down low, rumbling with the need to spill everything they had.

Yet the stallion could not hold back for a single moment more as he humped and ground, caught up in the desires of his body. With every stroke of his massive cock, he drove into the stoat's tail hole, stretching him out, forcing his body to pull and twitch and ache around him.

Letting loose came with a throbbing pulse of deep ecstasy, sending long, hot, thick spurts of cum deep into Cliff's backside. The stoat's tail sagged, no longer possessing the energy to keep it lifted out of the way, but that didn't matter with the massive girth stretching him out. Weakly, he tried to clench, but Cliff had to languish there, to take every drop, his stomach bloating out with the overload of seed.

A ragged whinny ripped itself from his nostrils as he heaved, leaning forward, his paws resting heavily on the stoat's hips. Dimly, he knew he had driven himself deeply enough into his partner's hole to get in that close to him, yet he was too caught up in the moment to consider anything else. It was just for him to experience, lusting in the moment, grunting deep in the back of his throat, his lips and nostrils quivering and twitching.

But he could only rest there, trembling in place, his balls tight with desire as he spent ropes of cream straight into the stoat. It had to go somewhere, pooling in Cliff's belly, inflating him deeply, from the inside out. His skin stretched easily over the massive load, growing to such a point that it pushed him off the ground, trying to tip him backwards so his head was higher while he had been on all fours before. Cliff squeaked and wiggled, laughing brokenly as he tried to catch his breath, limbs flailing.

"Agh!"

Mica was there to grab him, however, doing his best to steady him in place as he huffed and licked his lips, rolling waves of ecstasy pulling deep within his abdomen. Desire coursed through, like a beat he was destined to move to, and he gasped for air, ears splayed and need rolling deep within.

Yet it was there that Mica stayed as the stoat ballooned up, his stomach swelling, inflating even as his toes twitched and curled. Bigger and bigger until it was so swollen it was larger than the stoat's torso and lower half, including his legs, combined, comically fat with an overload of cum. Seed churned and sloshed around his squashy, overfilled belly, though all Cliff had was a low groan, panting heavily, trying to contain himself even in an overdose of pleasure.

It would all come well, his belly softening again as the effects of the transformation wore off, all returning to a normal state. Yet that was exactly the victory they all were hoping for, dimly and faintly returning to their reality of being up on stage, everything hanging out and on show. Still, of course, with Mica's heaving prick driven deeply up into the stoat's tail hole.

Yet they wouldn't have had it any other way, all with a little size gain to toy with, Mica patting Clifford's hip with a low chuckle.

"Let's do this again sometime, hm?"

Cliff moaned – which the stallion took as agreement.

In transformation, anything was possible. And that included pleasures untold too…

# Into the Ocean

Tim exhaled, standing on the shoreline, his toes curling into the damp sand. He smiled faintly, the sun shining, though he was the only one down there. That particular little beach was rather on the secluded side as there was an old, steep set of steps cut into the face of the cliff, leading him down, though it was dangerous after so much erosion. Not many could use it anymore and, well, he wasn't really supposed to either.

He just sort of, well…shimmied down the parts of the cliff that didn't have steps anymore. No big deal. Not when the cove was one of the last places Tim had to enjoy a special little ability that, well, had been a part of him for a few years at that point. It had taken his sexual awakening to unlock it, to bring forth a new aspect of his being, though he had not managed to grapple with his power until twenty-three, maybe twenty-four.

He exhaled, his long, blonde hair ruffled around his ears and down the back of his neck. It was a little messy and, of course, too long at that time, though the problem was that he just didn't have the time to get it cut. It just wasn't fun for him, sitting in the chair at the barbers, the snip-snip of the scissors going, hair falling around his shoulders and making a puddle of softness on the floor around his chair.

And the mirror… Yes, it was the mirror that he hated. Tim never spent much time looking at his reflection, though he knew he had dirty blonde hair, that he looked after, his eyebrows a little bushier than he would have liked. There wasn't much about him that really stood out, though he'd been asked out on a few dates and flirted with… Okay, so he knew he liked guys on that side, but that was about it, no more than that. But he didn't like how *he* was and had never felt like the person staring back at him in the mirror was, well, him.

That was why his powers had risen, showing him he was something else, someone else, entirely: a shapeshifter. Tim was yet to meet anyone who was a shapeshifter like him, but he'd seen flickers of them around the edges of society, things that didn't quite match up with what the norm was, people getting in tricky situations, up to places where they otherwise may not have been able to reach.

"Now…"

He breathed the word out, just a single word. There was no need for more, not as the Cornish breeze licked at his skin, playing with his hair.

Of course, Tim hadn't bothered putting any clothes on – well, he'd stripped off entirely at the base of the cliffs. Getting caught nude was not his concern, not as he breathed slowly and evenly, letting his desires course through him, pulse after pulse, throb after throb.

Sunshine glanced off his tanned skin. At the end of summer, he was comfortable in his skin, as long as he didn't spend too much time looking down at himself, even his shaft soft and balls exposed. Neither did those at all appear to be "his," not really, though he had never thought he was in the wrong body in terms of gender.

Ah… No. There was no sense in talking about anything like that when his heart yearned to take on his real form, his true form, what lay deep within him, as energy flickered to his fingertips.

Cool and sensual, it flickered and danced through him like sea salt on his lips, breathing deeply and evenly as his body slowly changed. His skin darkened, taking on bolder, more striking tones, his spine aching as it sought to shift.

*Here it comes…*

A sense of aching heaviness settled into him, as the pull of gravity was suddenly too much. That was why he needed to be out there, out in the water, and he wobbled as he took step after step forward, water bubbling around his toes as the foamy reaches of the waves stretched as far up the beach as the tide allowed. The pull of the tide, the magnetic reach that controlled it, was not something, however, that he had control over, even as a mere mortal.

As a shapeshifter, even then…Tim was still mortal. And that was okay too. He had everything he needed there before him, his skin darkening across his back and down his arms, while his belly faded to a pure, clean white. A crisp, sharp line differentiated between the black and white, two parts of an opposing force, but they blended together perfectly too, even as his body shifted.

A sea creature, after all, would need a layer of fat, called blubber, on their bodies to stay whole and healthy, to swim and move freely. It was not the warmest of climates, after all, off the coast of Cornwall, and it layered a thicker substance under his skin, keeping him from the chill of the outside air. It was still late summer, but it had not been the hottest of summers either, so the water would still be nice and cool for him.

Tim breathed as slowly and as evenly as he could, concentrating on how the flow of air felt sliding down his windpipe, into his lungs. Slowly but surely, his neck thickened a little and his nostrils flattened down, no longer needed on his face. There was one, heart wrenching moment where panic threatened to rise, where he was no longer able to breathe. And then a soft blowhole appeared at the back of his head, puckering and twitching as it gently exhaled a puff of air.

*Phew…*

That was always a tricky moment for Tim to go through, extending his arms out to either side of him, making a triangular shape with both of them, as if his head was the upper point of the triangle. There was not too much to change there, at least not outwardly, though his nails softened back down into his fingertips, no longer needed. He clenched his hands into fists and relaxed them again, his grip strength increasing a little more.

His skin was smooth, so very soon, so much so that he could practically glide his fingertips over it, as if there was a slick sheen there. Yet it was just the supple nature of his new skin at play, pliable and yielding enough that he could press his fingers into it for a moment, leaving an indentation. The indent jumped back the moment he released the pressure, of course, his body more than duly hydrated as he trembled and, slowly, strode out into the water.

His transformation swept over him a little more with every step, water splashing up around his legs, the sea foam lifting his heart more than even the sunshine could. Tim's hair retracted, itching and prickling as it drew back into his scalp, though it was always the sensation of the wind brushing his scalp that caught him the most during his transformations. It was not something he ever really got to feel otherwise, even if he had short hair at the time, wanting to bring his hands up to sweep over the increasingly round dome of his head.

That was alright though. It wasn't going to go anywhere in a hurry and he didn't need to yet relinquish his transformation, breathing deeply through his blowhole. It was still so strange, as sand squashed between his toes, offering him a greater level of grip as the water made its way up and over his hips, to feel his lungs working like that. He still thought, with muscle memory, that air was supposed to press up his windpipe and be inhaled and exhaled through his nostrils – but, of course, a blowhole was so much more efficient as a marine mammal.

Tim, however, would not lose his arms and legs during his transformation, not as a black bulge with a white underside throbbed from the base of his spine. No... He was a combination of animal and human, a hybrid that was called an anthro, to those in the know of that side of the world. Truthfully, he had not been until he had experienced his first transformation, which had come completely out of the blue.

One day, he would meet others that shapeshifted into anthros, just like him, and would be bold enough to see where the lines between them could be crossed. It was not right for him to live as isolated a life as he had.

Orcas, after all, were social creatures. They needed to be surrounded by the pod to feel whole, to have those connections and social relationships that were so important to them. It was only in transforming that Tim came to understand that.

His tail pressed out, the fluke slowly but surely forming as it extended out from the base of his spine. He tried to take a deeper breath but found his lungs shuddering, tighter than he would have liked them to be. It was okay though, as it was just the energy that the transformation demanded by him, pulse after pulse sinking into shifting his muscles and fat, forming fresh body matter where his tail grew.

It was interesting to have a tail and he puffed out his cheeks softly, his head rounding out smoothly like that of an orca's as his lips grew a little harder. Technically, they had a mouth filled with sharp teeth, though his teeth panged terribly as they narrowed into those more pointed tips for tearing into flesh.

Not that it mattered, even while he shook his head and strove to distract himself from the ache, his skull crackling as it enlarged. Although his organs changed size too, to fit a larger body, it was still not the most comfortable experience for him, no matter how many times he went through it.

He gulped as his neck thickened ever so slightly, though the addition of fresh weight on him was impossible to ignore. Shifting his weight back and forth, the transforming orca anthro slid his fingers, splayed out, down to his lower abdomen where his cock was slowly pulling back into his body.

That always unnerved him, but he felt so much better about that part of his body when it had fully transformed. To have his cock and balls out like that… Well, it simply felt unnatural, as if it was not right at all to have them all hanging out, wobbling around. The folds of skin didn't even look appealing to him and Tim breathed more easily as he watched them sink back into his body, his balls tugging up until they smoothed out again and there was no outward appearance of them even existing at all. Of course, he did not lose them, holding his testes internally instead, and his cock tucked itself away inside the slit at his lower abdomen. It would be there and ready whenever he needed it and he didn't have to worry about anything else in the interim.

It had never been a focus of his and he ran his fingers over the edge of his slit, though it folded back down into his body, so near to being close to seamless. He moaned softly and arched his back, pumping his hips forward as he invited his cock out once more. Sure, it had only just slipped inside, yet heat tickled his body, flowing through his veins as if need took the place of blood. There was so much more to be taken in the passion of transformation than what Tim had initially expected and he was more than willing to lean into it.

His smooth, slick body beckoned him as his hands splashed into the water, stroking his rising cock. Yet it was not anything that either a true orca or a human would have had: it was his version of both. The smooth, hot length throbbed into the light curve of his fingers, though it was perfectly soft with not a single bump or ridge on it. The tip tapered to a rougher, rounder point with a fat slit right at the head, designed as if to pry open a partner.

"Unff…"

Tim shuddered, his tail sweeping through the water, taking one shuddering step after the other, out into the water. The ocean was no foe to him, nothing to fear in the slightest, as he stirred up the sand around his feet and startled a stray ray, along with a couple of flatfish. The latter were more common in the Cornish shallows, though that was okay. He'd find far more when he struck out into deeper water, a creature of the ocean who moved on by without the concern of others. To the fish and the rays and more, he was just another creature, like them.

And that was just what Tim wanted, plunging underwater as the final nuances of his transformation settled into place. The biggest details he had to focus on came in the function at the front of his skull, where he sent his echolocation forth from. Seeing the pictures depicted in his head from sending out clicks would never cease to surprise him, though he wanted more than that.

The flow of water, as he swam, pumping his tail as the fluke fattened out, thickening and widening, stroked his cock, yet Tim didn't want to touch it. He'd given himself a touch of a tease and yet he wanted to be deeper, holding his breath, his blowhole instinctively closing at the brush of water pressure bearing down over it.

His body understood so much of what it had to do, even when he was not comfortable in that sort of world, not in a way he could have expected of himself. And yet with every trip out into the clear waters, striking out boldly from the comfort of the cove and the shoreline, Tim grew more confident, finding himself.

Who he truly was, after all, could not be acquired or achieved in the course of a single day, no. That was not how things were supposed to go, not as he swam back to the surface, breaching like an orca, his eyes a little strained as he blinked. Blinking was not as natural for an orca as it was for a human – but as a hybrid of both, he could do it more comfortably. He was glad of that, the reflex pulling at him, his tail swinging lightly back and forth until he leaned into the pressure of the muscle, pumping it up and down powerfully.

His own strength never failed to take his breath away as bubbles streamed around him and he sent out a series of clicks, painting an image in his head of the deeper seafloor, resplendent in rocks and a sea of kelp. It was one of his favourite directions in which to strike off into a dive for a reason, the powerful sweep of his tail drawing his attention more and more, pump after pump.

It was clear down there that day and he spared a passing look for a blue shark, though he was surprised to see one in shallower water. They were usually creatures of the deep, but some had been following the fishing boats of late too: anything for an easy meal.

Dimly, off in the distance, a pod of dolphins frolicked and clicked, but they were playing and not hunting; they wouldn't be interested in the anthro orca. He swam mostly with his tail, arms down by his sides for the time being, using the pump of his legs and tail together in a sort of dolphin or orca kick, smooth and fluid. If it felt easy to him, it was right. That was all Tim needed to know.

And yet the anthro orca did not know anything near enough about the world out in the water, not as he swam and turned, exhaling through his blowhole for the sheer thrill of swimming through the silvery stream of bubbles. He'd never tire of how they tickled and ran down his skin, prickling faintly, a sensation that simply could not be replicated in any manner when he was on land.

The water called to him – and then a silver-grey flash spun through his vision, streaking upward to break through the glittering barrier between water and sky.

The dolphin twisted and spun, like a spinner but they were spotted and splashed with freckles down their sides, as he flicked through the air, comfortable in his body. Yet he was not a dolphin that Tim would have expected to see out there, not like one of the pod members that were somewhere South-East of him.

He was an anthro just like him, with a longer, dolphin-like beak but still anthro features to the face and a dancing pair of glittering, blue eyes. Oh, even the sight of them had his heart doing a flip, a strong, slenderer tail fluke powering through the water to send him coursing easily through it.

Tim slowed, using his tail as an anchor to steady his pace a little, though the dolphin anthro was still on the move.

His first encounter with a shapeshifter... He breached again, powering up and sucking in a breath the moment he blew out, diving again swiftly to chase after them. The dolphin shifter was not far ahead, twisting and turning, and Tim would have blushed if he had possessed the ability to, for he had not retracted his cock during his swim. If he was honest, he didn't want it to slide away just yet – and he had thought he was on his own out there anyway! It wasn't his fault, no, that his cock was out and hard, showing off a little more than he could have expected to.

Sending a burst of echolocation clicks out, he followed the dolphin anthro, yet startled when an unknown presence brushed his mind.

*You seem eager to be out here.*

Tim gulped, pausing and floating upright in the water, his tail steadying him. Was that… Could that really have been the dolphin anthro, in his head? The words didn't feel like they belonged to him and, frankly, Tim never usually "thought" with words, his mind favouring images and impressions rather than the kind of mentality that could have a discussion with himself. Not everyone was the same in that regard either – which was why it stood out to him so much.

*You…* He tried hesitantly, reaching out mentally, not sure what he was doing. *Are you talking to me? Can I hear you? What are you doing?*

*Swimming, just like you.* The dolphin anthro said, swimming on his side and showing off his belly. Even though he was nude, he still looked presentable and modest – as his own cock was hidden within his belly slit. *But you seem to be enjoying it rather a lot more than I am. I must be missing out.*

The orca anthro clicked and turned away, but his shaft stubbornly remained out, lightly pink and fleshy. He half covered himself with his hands, ducking behind a rock. It would have to do for the moment as he hung out near the seafloor. What was done was done, however, and, strangely, there was not all that much embarrassment in him – more like a dim memory of how he thought he should have felt.

Tim parted his lips in a smile, stretching a little more at the corners.

*You're… You're like me,* he said, trying again to brush his mind with that of the other shapeshifter's. *Are you…*

*Yes, I'm a shapeshifter too. But I've not seen you out in these parts before. I'm Madid.*

The dolphin anthro grinned, clicking at him, turning and spinning in the water, a silvery stream of bubbles flowing from the blowhole on the back of his head. Tim exhaled, though he did not yet need to take in a breath, his tongue protruding out briefly, though that was not something either that he needed to do anymore.

Old habits, lifetime habits, died hard. But, eventually, Tim would get used to being in the body of a shapeshifter, an orca who was part creature and part human, an anthro hybrid of both, as they were called in lore and mythology.

*I'm Tim,* he said, feeling that he had to introduce himself too. *I… Hm. Sorry about my state. This is the first time I've seen anyone and…well, I said I wasn't expecting to meet anyone.*

*Oh, that's quite alright,* Madid said, swimming up to the other side of the rock. *It's easy to let go out here, isn't it?*

Tim nodded.

*It's not like being on land. It's like being…real.*

*I get that.*

Madid swam closer, forcing him back – but only because Tim was still trying to cover himself with his hands. The dolphin chuckled and chattered, parting his beak as bubbles streamed from his blowhole.

*Come on,* he teased softly, amusement brimming over as he touched Tim's mind with his own. *Mm… You've got to have a bit of fun with it too. Or would you rather head out to a little cove I know, sit and talk in the waves?*

It was hard to know what to say to that and Tim groaned. Decisions, decisions... The soft, logical part of him wanted to head out, to talk and to sit, to be modest again. But the orca didn't know of that side, sexually open, more liberated – yet still held back by the human side of him. Both parts had to work together and Tim grunted as he allowed Madid to swim up against him, fingertips gently brushing his shoulder, checking for permission.

*It's okay if you don't want to, you know,* he said, *explore a little more. Not everyone does. I've only met a finful of other shifters too.*

*Oh...* Tim smiled faintly, eyes resolute, meeting Madid's gaze. *Yes... Yes, I want to. But I don't really know what exactly you're proposing.*

The dolphin clicked and, with a flick of his tail and legs powering together, flipped over backwards, completing an underwater somersault while appearing as if it took no effort physically at all.

*Oh, wonderful... But all you need to do, if you want, is swim with me.*

That was easy. Easier. It was all Tim had wanted to do on diving into the ocean, on allowing all his changes to sink into him, flowing and ebbing, the rise and fall of the tides calling him on. Relinquishing his body to the sea, he swam swiftly to the surface for a quick breath, taking it with a sharp intake through his blowhole, and ducked down once more, following Madid.

Yet he didn't have to worry out there as the flow of water fluttering and teasing down the smooth, sinuous length of his body, muscles highlighted and defined, guided him on. His cock throbbed faintly and yet his eyes were on the dolphin anthro as he curved in close, flipping his tail fluke in a subtle brush against the orca's.

*Oh…*

*Isn't it wonderful?* Madid said, clicking again, his beak parted with sheer, dolphin-like joy. *You wouldn't recognise me in my human skin. But that's not really what this is all about, no…*

Madid showed him the way, like a current pulling him along with it, sweeping up against his body. Tim instinctively wanted to suck in a breath but, of course, could not while under the water, holding the tension in his lungs and reminding himself of where he was. Yet the smooth grind of Madid's body was more alluring still and he swore he could feel his cock pulsing, sending small spurts of pre-cum out into the ocean. If they were present, however, they dissipated too swiftly into the saltwater for him to even bear witness to them for even a moment.

*Swimming has never felt like this before,* he grunted, somehow feeling a tremor in his voice, even his mental voice. *You…*

*I'm here,* Madid reassured him, swimming more slowly, guiding Tim with the slow pump of his tail as they danced above the kelp beds, the softly fluttering fronds offering an additional sense of serenity. *Relax… Swim with me.*

Yet that was more and more difficult as Tim did all he could to swim, pumping his tail a little more fluidly, but not as much as he would have liked. Meeting another shapeshifter for the first time, well… He wanted to be smooth, powerful, calculating, showing off all of his body. Though perhaps not his cock…

Oh, even his thoughts weren't coming fluidly, though perhaps that too was for the better as Madid swam closer, keeping time with him, not even trying to power ahead. No, he kept pace with him, even letting the smooth expanse of his dolphin shifter body tease against Tim's soft skin.

He grunted, a stream of bubbles exploding in surprise from his blowhole, yet Tim didn't have time to consider anything more, not as need trembled through him. Heat simmered as if the very water around him was warming, though Tim was sure that could not be the case.

He just…wanted something. As if he was following the leanings of animal instinct, truly, for the first time, throwing caution to the waves, where it would be swept away. He didn't need to hold on to it anywhere near as tightly as he had, grunting thickly, as if something was tightening in his throat.

That was okay, however, as long as Tim relaxed, parting his lips slightly. It was okay also just to go with the flow, swimming more smoothly, more energetically, every pump of his tail fluke sweeping him through the water up against the dolphin.

And Madid's length eased out too, fully, the pink length with a soft undulation in it, though it was hard for Tim's eyes to focus on it when they were so close. If they had not been underwater, both mammalian anthros holding their breath, they would have been breathing heavily, yet there was a release to be had in the pressure of their lungs, of being aware they were underwater. They couldn't just flip back to the surface at any time, not when they wanted to be close, twining and twirling around one another, spinning and letting the current carry them.

*I feel you…*

Tim sent his thoughts out, the orca's lips parted softly, showing his teeth, though his lips quirked in a wondrous smile. He had to have it, had to let go, his body finding better use of his muscles when he wasn't thinking so much about what he was doing.

*And I feel you too,* Madid said gently, brushing his mind and letting it sit there, emotions tangling. *Let me know if anything is too much for you... You look amazing.*

It may well have been an interesting first encounter – but it was the encounter Madid and Tim had and would always remember, as they learned and grew as shapeshifters. The orca and the dolphin anthro spun around one another in a spiral of silvery bubbles, all streaming for the surface, even as their need came through, thick and full and fleshy and throbbing. Their cocks ground lustfully together as they swam and frotted into one another, the smooth, warm lengths grinding and humping. They didn't need to actively think about thrusting against each other, only letting their need thrum through, the pump of their tails more than enough to get them exactly where they needed to be.

Tim moaned, right where he wanted to be, even though it would take some time before his mind caught up to what was happening. Heat coiled tightly within him and, for the first time, truly, his cock throbbed in his anthro form. Even though Tim had got hard as an anthro, after transforming, before, he hadn't gone all the way.

That time was different – because he had Madid there with him, grinding and frotting, letting the slick slide of their shafts against one another take them forward, stroke by stroke. There was nothing else for either as the rest of the world, even the ocean, fell away, the teasing caress of water streaming over them both. He swore a shudder ran through the dolphin as he brought his hands up slowly to sweep them back down the dolphin's side, though it was fleeting and brief. It was left a moment he wanted to revisit all over again, coming back to it just to see what he could lust for, long for, taking for himself.

Yet it would be shared too with the other shapeshifter as he moaned aloud, the soft tenor of his voice vibrating through the water. Tim let it all roll through him, throb after throb, pulse after pulse, relishing in his body, the form that he was only just coming to understand and appreciate.

And yet it was the twitch of Madid's cock against his that did it for him, even as the dolphin chattered and swung his beak back and forth, ejaculating forcibly, long spurts of seed flooding the water, only to be carried away a moment later. It could not linger there, not even a rich, hot rush of need swelled through Tim, his cock twitching, feeling like it was trying to get even closer to the dolphin's shaft.

*Mmmm… Madid…*

He let go, completely and utterly, spending his seed, though it felt as if his form settled even more around him, with that ejaculation. His seed flooded the water – and yet it was not enough to impact the ocean. Not even their transformed bodies would, sharing space with it, relaxing and releasing there, though only time would say quite how their relationship would develop.

Into the ocean, they went, together, side by side, their cocks still hard and throbbing. Ready for more the dolphin and orca anthros swam, giggling and spinning, tails twirling, showing off all their shifted forms could do.

They had all they needed, out there.

And, finally, in each other too.

# Hybridisation

I knew it was going to come, sooner or later, but, well… I didn't think it was going to be that striking. As a gryphon, I was already a hybrid of crow and black panther, following the usual lineage of many in my family – but there was a broken gene, apparently, in my genealogy. That was the ability…to not quite hold on to my form.

So, I changed. One day. I didn't know when that day was going to come, but, once it did, there turned out to be nothing I could do about it. I was just there, stuck, frozen in the middle of the street, a plastic shopping bag swinging from my paw-like hand, as if I had turned into a statue.

There were no warnings as to what was to happen, my breath barely coming, trapped in the back of my throat. I grunted and wheezed, feeling as if my eyes were bulging, barely even able to blink, my shoulder blades pushed back.

*Ah… Damn it…*

A new form was coming and there was nothing at all I could do about in the blustery, wet, Autumn weather. My hood whipped back from my head as rain pattered over my skull, my already sleek, black feathers gleaming with moisture, shining softly. And yet it was not my place to be there, to witness it, not as something pulled between my legs, a chill running through me.

I would have closed my legs and squeezed my thighs around the slit there, though it was not the case. A male would often, after all, try to protect what lay down there, even if my testes were internally held at that time. That was okay though, something I'd grown up with, even after reaching maturity, and I groaned softly in the back of my throat, though it was more like an exhale than any sound I recognised.

Whether I was ready for it or not, it was happening, my arms stiff and unwieldy, no longer mobile. Slowly, too slowly, my fingers uncurled and the shopping I'd forget about in a little while spilled on to the pavement, fruit bouncing along in a flash of red for an apple while a banana rolled into the gutter. But it didn't matter, worry tangling with excitement as my stomach lurched and my legs, slowly but surely, thickened.

It was more noticeable to me than it was to my clothes, however, the muscle growing more defined and coming up quickly against the limits of my jeans, fighting the seams. I shifted my weight the little I was able and tried to bear through it all the best I could, huffing and grunting, resisting the urge to lick the edge of my narrower beak. My tongue was more flexible, of course, than that of a typical crow, but it was not a natural motion.

Nothing was natural as my shoulders broadened, my jacket protesting, cutting in under my arms as my body shifted, laying down muscle where there had been none before. I was typically quite slim – but all was about to change as I tumbled over the precipice, one body exchanged for another.

There would be no going back to my crow-panther gryphon form, not truly, and I closed my eyes against the knowledge of that, the grey sky swirling above me with scudding clouds. The wind picked up, damp, Autumn leaves fighting its grasp, yet it was not their place at all to battle back against the change, not any more than it was my place to fight what had befallen my family for generation after generation.

"Okay..."

I breathed out the word as a form of acceptance, opening my eyes again, moist with tears. But it was okay, it was truly okay. I had expected it and the transformation was coming, whether I leaned into it or restrained myself.

So, I allowed my shoulders to broaden, a little movement returning to my limbs, enough so that I could twitch and raise my arms slightly while adjusting the stance of my hind paws. Of course, I had custom-made boots to protect them from the streets, the damp and the grime, but even those felt too tight around my paws, claws curling down, trapped for space.

My jacket pulled and pulled and pulled and I would have taken it off if I'd had the chance to, though that was just one more thing stripped from me. To gain, I had to lose: and there was a lot of me to lose first, in the shedding of that form.

I grunted, my beak softening, oddly so, coming down into a somewhat mammalian muzzle, though it felt longer than what I may have expected. It was difficult to discern, running my fingers up and along it, and I whimpered throatily, a bubble of emotion making its way all the way up to my lips.

"Oof…"

The beak was a part of me and yet it had to go, more sensation coming to my lips as they formed. I tried to open and close my mouth, the hinge of my jaw foreign to what I was used to, lips spreading back and back and back, as if I was to have a very long muzzle indeed.

It was something, at least, and I relished the notion of being able to chew properly for the first time, the hardness of the beak finally slipping away as a prickling crackle rolled through my skull. There didn't seem to be many changes to be made there, more or less keeping the shape of it, though black feathers fluttered from me as my skin itched and tugged and pulled.

I brought my hand to my neck where feathers puffed away in a black deluge, my skin beneath turning leathery, almost scaley – but not there yet. Almost without thinking about it, I turned my head from the left to the right and back again, working out new muscles as my neck lengthened, just a little, my skull popping faintly as new vertebrae were added.

A hole in the back of my jeans allowed my leonine tail out, yet it thickened slowly, filling the gap that had been made to allow it free. Yet that was not quite where my attention was due as I took another shuddering breath, my chest rising, expanding, muscles swelling to fill out my pectorals and, even lower, my abdominal muscles too.

I stood taller, pushing up on to my toes, the world around me seeming strange. Was I bigger? It was hard to say, even though the pavement looked further away than before, the fish and chip shop a little further down the road flashing its neon sign. It buzzed and flickered, as if the electricity had a fault in it somewhere, but that wasn't any of my concern.

I swayed, needing to balance. My feet moved, but each step was huge and lumbering, as if I had forgotten how to walk. I was struck by the ridiculousness of that and warbled a bubbling, strangled kind of laugh, shaking my head. To think that I had forgotten how to walk? How would that even work?

I didn't know, but I'd have to learn, my black wings hanging down loosely, limply, though I was at the very least relieved to still feel their weight on my back: a comforting presence. I had to get to the side, away from the street, even though it was quiet even of cars passing by. All I'd been doing was trying to walk home after a quick trip to the shops, but things had gone terribly askew that day. All I wanted was to get home in one piece to my little flat, so I could hunker down and take in the depths of my transformation.

*Alleyway…* I thought, though even my thoughts felt as if they came a lot more slowly and sluggishly than before, as if they were being drawn through slick, heavy sludge. *Got to…get…somewhere…quiet… Quiet…alleyway…*

It was not far, but it may as well have been a mile, shuffling across the ground, the hard bottoms of my boots scraping the pavement. A few steps, slowly, barely lifting my foot: they got me closer, the narrow alleyway seeming to go behind a row of shops in a little community shopping area, with a little supermarket too. It would have to do.

With a great effort of will as more feathers fell out from the bottom of my T-shirt, I stepped heavily, my hind paw coming down with a lot more pressure than strictly necessary. My tail fattened, more muscles controlling it, with more flex in it than the panther's tail had ever given me, unusually so. My wings felt strange, like something was peeling from them, though I put it down, at least for the moment, to the feathers spilling from those too.

Oh, I would miss my feathers…

Staggering into the alleyway as another transformation pulled at me, I tripped over my own feet, my tail twisting and curling behind me: snake-like, and entirely with a mind of its own. It was much, much thicker than anything a creature I recognised should have had, as if I had become a hybridisation of a third creature too, not only split as a gryphon was.

No… I was to become something so very much more than any gryphon who had gone before me. And that was okay too. Not everything in the world, namely my body and transformations, was ever meant to be within my control.

"Come… Unff…"

I could barely get words out as I leaned heavily into the wall, a window in the back of one of the shops showing me the oddly grotesque creature I was, midway through transformation. It was not a scaled layer coating me, as I'd suspected, but leathery skin, like that of a reptile. Yet there was no confusing the horns aching from the back of my head, laying down fresh bone to form them, for anything else – not with the longer, almost elegantly narrow muzzle that had formed.

My face was not mammalian, no… But draconian, a dragon's snout, just with the mammalian flexibility that so many anthros tended to enjoy. I flicked my tongue out as it thinned down even more, becoming serpentine, yet parted my lips with a strangled gulp of horror as it split.

Right down the middle, one tongue became two, and I trembled as new nerve endings were laid down, a passive player in my own transformation. Yet that left me free to feel everything, to take in even the little details as my wings finally lifted, separating in a funny way.

I flicked my new second tongue around my mouth, though both tongues were still connected at the root, which was something I could work with, at least. Still, it was weird to run both tongues around the inside edges of my growing teeth at once, instead of the edge of a beak. Fangs lined my muzzle, suited to a dragon, mostly canines with some rougher molars right at the back.

Would I be able to breathe fire? Maybe those molars were for striking the fire, like striking flint on a rock back when I had been camping… That was something, however, I'd come to see another time.

My wings, however, had to be considered too as I turned side-on to the dirty reflection, barely able to see anything at all – but it was better than nothing. And it distracted me too from the dull, throbbing ache of new teeth pushing from the bone of my jaw, making me grunt and shudder with a whole-body ripple going through me. My wings didn't look like wings anymore, my leathery hide taking on a blue-green tint as they fanned out into four pieces. It didn't look like they would be usable as wings anymore either, not for flying, and something pulled inside me, sinking, to leave the sky behind.

I would, however, gain something else as my wings stretched with a slick, shiny material between the spokes of them. It didn't feel like skin, not in any way that I was familiar with, though it fanned out between the growing spines of my wings like what I'd expect to see in a dragon's body. But it was different, definitely so, glistening even in the low, dull light of the afternoon, the wings shifting a little, controlled by muscles at the base.

For they were not wings but *fins*, I thought, gulping hard, my tongues working together to push saliva to the back of my mouth without me even having to think about it. They were like the fins of fish – or sea dragons, though I had never had the good fortune to meet one.

Yet it only then came to my attention that I was not losing the fur from the panther part of my body, but losing the colour alone as it thickened up, fluffing out the bottom of my jeans as my boots creaked around my feet. They were good quality, though I'd had them for a few years, and I was loathe to lose them even as black claws poked out the front, sharp and demanding space to grow into. My feet were larger, as if they were to tread quietly over surfaces without making a sound

– though I didn't know all that much about mammals in the world, only researching the history, particularly, of my own anthro kind.

I'd soon see that there was so much more to me, however, so much I could not have realised lay dormant, as white fur thickened up around my legs, soft and fluffy, brushing against my skin where my clothes trapped it. Yet my boots gave up completely as my toes wriggled out the front, having been made way for by my claws. I tried to clench them a little, scrunching up my toes, though I did not yet have full dexterity there.

As a hybrid dragon-wolf-snake, I settled into my new form with a weight upon me, though I was easily two feet taller than I had been. It was a miracle my clothes covered up anything at all, though my jeans had crawled up my legs, exposing the white wolf fur, those big paws exploding through my shoes. There was not all that much that had changed about my stance, which was gratefully received, but I was covered with far more muscle than before, power rippling through me.

Oh, how I wanted to see what that power could do, even as my hand swept down my body, feeling my chest and then my stomach through the tight, stretched fabric of my clothes. My lower belly was exposed and I twisted, further ripping my jacket, though it gave me some relief from where it was pulling across my shoulders and upper back. Leathery skin changed to white fur down there, though I hadn't expected it to draw up so high on my body. Especially with the leathery skin framing my upper half.

But maybe that was just how it was meant to be and I had to go along with it, letting the transformation rip through me, panting heavily as my claws dug into the wall, the blue-green, leathery skin wrapping around the back of my hand, appearing rougher around the wrist. Maybe that was from when I had that injury when I was younger, leaving a scar there and scuffed-up feathers?

I'd find that out in time, even as my groin ached deeply, something pulling within me that I had to follow the line of. I had to take the lead of the transformation, my lips trembling into a grin, though I didn't need to glance in the reflective window anymore. It was too dirty to really take in my full form and figure, after all, and it was better to feel.

The fur warmed me, though I tugged helplessly at my clothes, fabric straining and stretching, buttons popping off the jacket as the shirt beneath ripped up the seams. I had to get it off, one way or the other, and my claws, at the very least, made quick work of it. Having my bare chest out was not the worst, though a chill of exposure still rolled through me, even though I was tucked away back in the alleyway.

Hopefully, no one would see me there, though it was not as if I could stop the transformation if I wanted to. I ran my twin tongues around my mouth again, marvelling at the teeth, how things were changing so very much, things that would affect my daily life even if it was not something I'd considered before. And that tail... It was strange, more like the body of a snake than a dragon's tail, the tip round and bulging, something like a head. Yet there were no eyes on it, nor nostrils nor a mouth. There wasn't anything at all there to make it look like a snake, as much as it shuddered and rippled and twisted, but I still figured it to be such.

Dragon... Mammal... And snake. I wasn't sure what the mammalian part of me was, the one with fluffy, thick white fur, but it didn't seem like a polar bear. It was warm but not that warm, for cold weather creatures had special hair on their body, ones that insulated and waterproofed them. I remembered that snippet of information from way back in my days of school, though I was several years out of school by that point.

It was funny the things we remembered, even when they didn't bear any significance anymore in our daily lives.

Yet there was something that drew my attention down, my jeans biting up between my legs in a way I didn't want to acknowledge, not in the slightest. But something had to give as I shifted my weight back and forth, adjusting my stance, feeling a little more natural if I tipped forward slightly. But maybe that too was me just trying to make sense of things and balance myself, when my whole world was reeling beyond any form of mental comprehension.

I exhaled, chancing it as heat rushed to my leathery cheeks, though my skin clung to me, offering my face and muzzle shape and definition. I hoped it was elegant, though my muzzle was definitely on the narrower side, even if the horns were thickening where they attached to my skull, offering a wider, flared base.

But the jeans had to come off as I sliced through them as delicately as I could with the sharp claws. Those would have to be filed down, sooner or later, but I'd have to get by for at least a few days with them while I worked out how to care for my new body. For as long as I had it, at least.

"Oof…"

I grunted, licking my lips, the wet slap of two tongues awkward to control, yet that heat between my legs begged attention – and I wasn't so sure it was just because of the pressure of my clothes cutting off the circulation. No, there was warmth swirling and pooling between my legs, breath leaving me in soft, heady pants.

There had only been a slit where my shaft had been tucked away before, displaying more avian-gryphon attributes, but my body twitched and shivered as a sheath formed, my clothes shoved down only far enough to expose it. And even that was too much for me, grunting and heaving, great, dragging breaths clawing at my lungs in the worst of ways.

Out, in… Out…in… I tried to slow my breathing, concentrating on each and every breath filling my lungs as if they were the only important thing in my life. I took a trembling breath, a contracting ripple running through me, but that new fold of flesh, my sheath, tingled as something pushed from it.

And what emerged was not like any cock I had seen before – at least, not in my experience. Which was limited, kind of, but that was not really something I worried about, not before. I hissed through my new teeth as a red shaft swelled from it, the white of the sheath standing out in stark contrast to it, though the moment did not highlight it as much as I wanted it to, cast into the dim shadow around my crotch. An absent-minded claw sliced away just a little more of my jeans, allowing more to reveal itself, but my throbbing cock had a mind of its own.

It was wolf-like – kind of. But there was no fat knot at the base, not even soft and uninflated, but bumps like barbs lining the length. They were not like the ones felines would have had in times gone by, the ones that would be sharp, catching and raking through a partner's hole. No… They seemed softer and springier as I ran my trembling fingers over them, barely able to believe that the cock was mine. But sensation won out as I stroked it, running the tip of a finger, careful of the claw, around the nodules, the bumps and soft, flexible barbs, the base of my dick seeming wider and flared – kind of like the base of my horns.

"Oh…"

The word came out slurred, whispering into a moan, but it was only me there to hear it and nothing else to concern myself with, no, not at all. I knew I was exposed there, even as the rain picked up a little, pattering down around me and cooling the exposed parts of my body, shifting my weight in my ripped and ruined boots. But I couldn't stop myself, my hand returning to my cock even as I tried to tug my fingers away from it, to have some manner of self-control.

I needed it, as my tail whipped back and forth, the round tip heavy, like a club. But it would come to me in time as the wing-fins on my back extended a little more, flapping and waving back and forth, like they were trying to shape the air. But they would shape water far better than they ever would tease their way through the air – and flight was something that had been taken from me, without my will to do so.

Maybe that was why I leaned into the warming ecstasy, breaking from my own sense of loss. My spine crackled as it lengthened again and my tail helped me balance too, though it didn't seem to want to stay still in the slightest, as if it was a separate part of me with a mind wholly of its own.

I had to play my fingers and palm over my cock, the size growing, though it seemed in proportion to my body still. It swelled a little, filling my hand, I groaned: a deep, guttural sound.

"Mmmm…"

Oh, it was good, so very good. And it was much, much better to lean into that and to embrace my new body and life to the best of my ability. I squeezed the base, marvelling at how my fingers only just closed around it, though it pressed my fingers apart more and more, as if that would not be the case for all that much longer. I tipped my shoulder into the wall, resting there, though it was not comfortable in the slightest. My wings shifting pulled at the clothing left across my back and shoulders, but a water dragon – at least that part of me – would not fare well with that restriction.

The world would see me as a hybrid, maybe even something of a freak... But they were going to have to make of me what they would, for I was who I was, one way or the other.

"Mmmph... Yes..."

Words came a little more easily, working the split tongue in my mouth carefully to push them out. It was still difficult not to drool around a tongue like that, one or two tongues – oh, it was hard to work out just how to refer to them. Yet that didn't matter, no, not as I whimpered throatily, a bubble of emotion bursting in my throat.

"Nnngghhh..."

A deeper groan still rolled from my lips – and, just like that, I lost the thought. It slipped away, far too easily, but my mind was on pleasure, on just how my cock pulsed within my hand.

And, finally, as my transformation settled over me, it came to light there was one bit of me left to change. Of course, my testes had still been there, but they had to descend, slowly and surely filling out a heavy, furry sack, clad in that same white fur as my lower half. I moaned, tongues dangling from my mouth, beyond my control, and teased one finger over them lightly.

My new balls... Oh, I had wondered just how they would feel, how sensitive they would be, needing to feel them, the weight of them, even as they swayed faintly and wobbled, filling out with need and cum. I arched my back, pumping my hips without thinking about it, everything falling into place and simply coming naturally.

Even with fur covering them, a softer, lighter coat of it protecting them, my balls were tended to and I hissed wetly as need coursed through. Pressure drove me on, panting softly, and I lusted for that high, the twist and pull of need in the pit of my stomach foreign and yet comforting.

It came with a promise, yes... A promise of ecstasy. And I only had to be bold enough to take that trembling high for myself, pumping the full length of my cock with one hand, trying my best to lock into the moment. If I forgot the rest of the world, perhaps I could finally be myself, letting the bump of my hand grinding over the soft "barbs" carry me away.

Sensation was king and I moaned aloud, shaking my head, somehow ducking forward against the wall. I didn't know how I'd got there, though it'd been the weight of my new balls that had broken me, panting heavily, every breath heaving through my chest as if it took a lot more effort to claim than it actually did.

My tail swung back and forth, settling now that I was giving it exactly what it wanted, that pleasure, that stability, feeding that desperate need. I tried to lick my lips, though it only added more wetness to them and the side of my muzzle, my teeth fine and sharp – fish-catching teeth.

But I needed that aching high, working my hand back and forth more and more fervently, grunting deep in the back of my throat. A rippling shudder ran through my tail and I gulped, eyes half-closed, rain cooling my body.

I was where I needed to be, even if I was not where I wanted to be. Everything would have been so much easier if I'd transformed while I'd been home, but there was no way to change how things had ultimately panned out. Pleasure warmed me, rising through my body to my skin from the inside out, panting increasingly heavily, my wing-fins shuffling back and forth. It was hard to pump my cock, not with the barbs getting in the way, but I had to do it, had to keep going.

I just had to think of what I wanted and follow it with all the longing in my heart. Orgasm clawed at me, driving me on: a feral, primal urge that made me want it all the more. There was nothing quite like it, though I could never have expected just how rampant it would me, how it would swell through me, filling me up as if a slick, hot fluid was being poured into be, making me yearn whole-heartedly for more.

So much more… And I was so much more than I had been, licking my lips, rolling my shoulders, even turning my head back and forth in a futile effort to contain the need vibrating through me. That desire could not be turned off, no, and neither did I want to quell it, not as the alleyway became the settlement of my transformation.

As a hybrid, a blend of three species, I moaned loudly, moisture in the corners of my eyes. Yet they were not tears, rather an accumulation of emotion that had to come out, my hand working more swiftly over my cock, the throbbing pulse guiding me on and on and on. Pre-cum trickled over my hand as my dick flexed within my hand and I thrust into it, finally falling.

Yet the groan that ripped itself from my lips was raw and carnal and spoke of times beyond my understanding. Cum shot from my cock as throbs of devout pleasure claimed me, stealing my breath from my lungs and any words from my lips. I rocked my hips, thrusting into my hand, yet the moment was for me and me alone, exulting in the selfishness of the act.

My seed splattered the wall as I rolled through my high, letting it come, enjoying the moment. The aftermath would be for me to clean up, even if the rain would wash away most of my cum from where I marked the wall and alleyway floor, a breathless laugh clutching at my throat. Sagging forward, I braced myself, weakly, on the wall with one hand, even though there was so much more to my transformation and life to understand in that moment, pressing on through bone-shaking waves of delight.

"Mmmm…"

I paused there, letting everything sink in. There was no rush, even though I wanted to get home, even though I wanted to be in the privacy of my own home. I could let the weight of my new body hold me, support me, though only experience would tell just how I could use the wing-fins.

In hybridisation, there were endless opportunities.

I only had to be bold enough to take them for my own. Even when my cock was softening gently in my hand, my cream dripping down the wall. It was dirty and it was messy and, as a trembling smile caught my lips, I knew I was going to be okay.

As long as I was me, I would always be okay.

Thank you for reading and I hope that these little stories were thoroughly enjoyed, giving you a little break to read and relax!

Are you ready for more? Check out my author website for more furry fiction and where you can purchase my books!

https://linktr.ee/amethystmare

Cover art illustrated by Kai_art; they are contactable via e-mail for work enquiries.

dongvieck10@gmail.com

www.ingramcontent.com/pod-product-compliance
Lightning Source LLC
Chambersburg PA
CBHW030025200726
48283CB00012B/1015